The Riddle of
Holiday House

Enid Blyton

The Riddle of Holiday House

AWARD PUBLICATIONS LIMITED

This book was first published in Great Britain
under the title *Holiday House* by Evans Brothers Ltd
in 1955. It was updated and altered to become part
of the Riddle series in 1997 by Enid Blyton's
daughter, Gillian Baverstock.

For further information on Enid Blyton
please visit *www.blyton.com*

ISBN 978-1-84135-737-9

Illustrated by Patricia Ludlow
Cover illustration by Gavin Rowe

First published 1955 as *Holiday House*
Revised edition published 1997 as *The Riddle of Holiday House*
First published by Award Publications Limited 2004 as
The Young Adventurers at Holiday House
This edition entitled *The Riddle of Holiday House*
first published 2009

Published by Award Publications Limited,
The Old Riding School, The Welbeck Estate,
Worksop, Nottinghamshire, S80 3LR

10 2

Printed in the United Kingdom

CONTENTS

CHAPTER 1

A Splendid Idea

"There!" said the doctor, slapping Nick on the back. "That's the last time I shall be seeing you, young man. You and your sister are absolutely fine now."

"Oh, good," said their mother. "But they look so pale and thin and neither of them has much of an appetite. Do you think they should go away somewhere, Doctor Hibbert?"

"Well, yes, Mrs Terry, I do," said Dr Hibbert. "But aren't you off to America with your husband? I wouldn't want them to go on an exciting trip like that – they need to laze about by the sea while they get their energy back."

"Oh, great!" said Nick. "We can easily go somewhere on our own, Mum. We're very good at taking care of ourselves."

"Oh, are you?" said his mother. "This year, between you, you've had one broken arm, one sprained ankle, one lost bicycle and one broken camera!"

She turned to the doctor.

"I'll arrange something," she said. "I've heard of a very nice holiday place down by the sea in Devon where unaccompanied children can go. I'll see if they'll have them."

"Can we take Punch?" Katie asked anxiously. "He wouldn't like having to stay behind with Gran."

"Yes, I think you'll be able to take him," said her mother. "I know this holiday place takes pets, too." She turned back to Dr Hibbert. "Well, Doctor, thank you for all your care and trouble – and, much as I like you, I do hope we shan't see you here again for a very long time, except on a friendly visit!"

Dr Hibbert laughed, said goodbye and went off in his car.

The two children looked at one another in delight. Nick was ten and tall for his age, with dark brown hair. Katie, who was nearly nine, looked very like him although her hair was a lighter brown and straight. They exchanged broad grins.

"Won't it be wonderful to have a holiday all by ourselves?" said Katie.

"Great!" said Nick. "Mum, tell us about this holiday place."

"Well, all I know about it is that it's called Holiday House and it's run by a Mrs Holly. It's quite near the sea, almost on the beach, in fact, and the food is very, very good," said Mrs Terry. "The Knott children went there, and they loved it."

"I hope they'll be able to take us in at short notice – and Punch too," said Katie. "Do write straight away, Mum."

"I think I'll telephone," said her mother. "I've got the number somewhere. I'll do it now."

"That's the great thing about you, Mum – you always do things at once!" said Nick approvingly. "You never put anything off, do you?"

"I wish I could say the same of you two," said Mrs Terry, looking in the desk for her address book. "Ah – here it is."

She was soon on the telephone and in a minute or two was talking to Mrs Holly. The children stood nearby, listening. It seemed as if it would be quite all right for them to go to Holiday House!

"Very well," they heard their mother say. "I will send them down tomorrow. They've had chickenpox very badly, then they caught that nasty flu bug and couldn't seem to throw it off. I'm afraid they've been rather spoilt for six or seven weeks – and they're always a bit of a handful, anyway. I hope they won't be too much trouble – they're good at heart, really! Send them straight back if they make a nuisance of themselves!"

"Oh, Mum," groaned Nick. "You don't need to say all that, you really don't!"

"Shh," said his mother, and turned back to the telephone to finish her conversation. She put down the receiver and smiled at the two children.

"Well – that was quickly arranged, wasn't it? Now I'll help you pack. You need to take some books, a pack of cards and some games. That's all in the amusement line. And we mustn't forget swimming things."

"Oh – will we be allowed to swim?" said Katie, pleased. "I thought you'd say, 'You mustn't do this, you mustn't do that. You've been ill, you must be careful.'"

"Oh, you're quite all right now," said her mother. "And, anyway, Mrs Holly is used to having children after they've been ill. I don't expect she'll stand any nonsense!"

"Is she nice, do you think?" asked Nick. "I don't want to be ordered about, and told to do this and go there. I hate that."

"It won't hurt you not to be spoilt for a bit," said his mother, laughing. "Heavens, to think of all the hours I've read to you and Katie lately, and the games I've played on your untidy beds, and the lost things I've hunted for in the bedclothes – honestly, I think I need a holiday myself!"

"You've been great," said Katie, suddenly realising how patient and kind her mother had been. She gave her a quick hug. "You have a good time in America, Mum – and don't you worry a single minute about us! I'll look after Nick and see that he behaves himself."

Nick looked at her indignantly. "Look after me! I like that! Boys look after girls, not the other way round. I'll see that Katie doesn't do anything silly, Mum."

"Now, now, don't start squabbling," said his mother, seeing Katie's face looking indignant. "Come and help me pack."

It was fun packing to go away and, as usual, it was very, very difficult to choose which books to take, and what games. Katie tried on her swimsuit and announced that it was much too small. Nick said the same, and pranced about the bedroom looking ridiculous in very, very tight swimming trunks.

"We'll go down to the shops and get a few things," said Mrs Terry. "You both want new sandals, I see."

"Yeah!" yelled Nick, catching Katie's hands and whirling her round the room. Punch leaped round them both, barking in excitement.

By bedtime, everything was packed and ready. The children were almost too excited to sleep. Punch, the terrier, had caught the excitement too, and had rushed about all day long, barking and getting into everyone's way.

"It's brilliant that Holiday House takes dogs, Punch," said Katie, giving the little dog a hug. "I wouldn't have gone without you. Mum, are we going to take Punch's basket?"

"No," said Mrs Terry. "I expect Mrs Holly will have an old cushion she'll lend you. She's used to taking pets. Now do go to sleep."

The next day was bright and sunny, and the children were up early.

"We've got to go round and say goodbye to everything," said Nick.

His grandmother overheard him, and laughed. "Goodbye to the dolls, goodbye to Mike and Penny next door, goodbye to the horse in the field, goodbye to me, goodbye to the gardener, goodbye to—"

"Don't laugh, Gran," said Katie. "I bet you used to say goodbye to everything before you went away when you were young. We always do. Oh – are those biscuits for us?"

"Yes. To eat in the train," said Gran, putting them into a bag. "And mind you behave yourselves, now – no hiding in cupboards at Holiday House and jumping out suddenly like you did yesterday! I'll miss you both, you rascals!"

"We'll send you a postcard," promised Nick, giving her a bear hug. "There's Mum calling, Katie. Come on, it's breakfast time."

Mrs Terry put them in the train after breakfast and asked the guard to keep an eye on them. He was a grumpy old fellow with sharp eyes under shaggy eyebrows. He nodded his head.

"Aye, I'll keep an eye on them. And if they get up to any nonsense I'll lock them into my van! Where are they to get out, did you say? Oh – Tolly Halt. Right, I'll see to them."

It was quite a long way in the train. Mrs Terry had packed them up a good lunch, and they ate it far too soon, so that they were hungry again long before they came to Tolly Halt.

"Look – there's the sea! Surely that's the sea!" said Katie, pointing to a bright blue streak in the far distance. "We must be nearly there!"

"Hurray!" cried Nick. "I can't wait to swim and climb cliffs and explore the countryside."

Soon the blue streak was a wide, sparkling expanse of water. The children suddenly felt excited. A holiday – all on

their own – nothing to do all day long but
bathe and paddle and row and fish!

The train began to lose speed and drew
slowly into the station. Then it came to a
halt by the platform, and Katie put her
head out of the window.

"Nick! It's Tolly Halt! This is where we
get out. Quick!"

Nick opened the door and they jumped
out. At the back of the train they saw the
guard pulling out their two suitcases. He

saw them getting out and called to them.

"Here you are – Tolly Halt. There's someone to meet you over there." He pointed to the far corner of the station.

The children looked round with Punch, the terrier, leaping round their legs on his lead. They saw a small car not far off, standing in the narrow road that led to the Halt. In it was a woman who waved to them, and a small girl. The woman called out cheerfully, "Are you Nicholas and Katie? I've come to meet you. I'm Mrs Holly. Can you manage those suitcases?"

"Oh, yes," said Nick, and the children took a case each. Punch pulled at the lead, eager to stretch his legs after the long train journey.

They walked to the car, while the train slid away from the Halt and disappeared into the distance.

"Hello!" said a sharp little voice. It belonged to a small girl of about eight, who looked them up and down. "I'm Clare. This is my mother. You have to get in the back."

Mrs Holly smiled at the children. "Welcome to Tolly Sands," she said. "I hope you'll have a lovely time here!"

CHAPTER 2

Holiday House

The children shook hands with Mrs Holly, who had a pleasant face with bright red cheeks and hair the colour of corn. Her eyes were very blue as she smiled at them.

"She's nice – but, as Mum would say, 'There's no nonsense about her!'" thought Katie as she got into the car. "We'll have to be careful, or she'll be after us properly."

Mrs Holly's daughter, Clare, watched the children from her seat beside her mother, her eyes as sharp as her voice! She missed nothing. "The dog mustn't sit on the car seat, must she, Mum?" she said. "She must get down."

"She's a he, not a she," said Nick. "And, anyway, he's not on the seat. He's on my knee. He's on his best behaviour."

"He looks a lively little dog," said Mrs Holly, driving off from the station. "What's his name?"

"Punch," said Katie. "We called him after a little terrier that we saw in the circus, who was very clever and could do lots of tricks."

"We've tried to teach Punch to beg and to walk on his hind legs, but he just wants to play," said Nick. "He's still only nine months old so maybe he'll be easier to teach when he's a bit older."

"I've got a cat at home," said Clare, in her sharp little voice. "A big tom-cat, black as soot, called Gruff. He doesn't mind dogs a bit."

"He's used to them," said Mrs Holly. "He'll soon be playing with Punch."

"Er – well, I hope you're right," said Nick. "Punch sometimes chases cats."

"He won't chase Gruff," said Clare at once. "No dog has ever chased Gruff. You can't chase a cat that doesn't run away. Gruff just sits down firmly and refuses to move."

"Are there any other children at Holiday House, Mrs Holly?" asked Katie.

"Yes," said Clare, answering before her mother could get a word in. "There's dear, darling Vicki and her sniffy nanny, and there's Jamie, the ugliest baby you ever saw, and there's John, who's going tomorrow – he's a nuisance."

"That's enough, Clare," her mother said sharply. "You're not to talk like that. I've told you before."

Clare took no notice. "And there's a very big boy called Gareth. I call him Gloomy Gareth."

"Why?" asked Nick, rather amused with all this chatter from Clare.

"Well – because he's gloomy, of course," said Clare. "He's a bookworm too – he sits with his nose buried in books all day long, he never plays a game, and he never smiles."

"Oh, Clare, how you do jabber!" said her mother. "Don't take any notice of her tongue, children – it runs away with her. Gareth isn't really gloomy – he's just working very hard for an exam. He's fifteen. He had a tutor who stayed here, to help him, but he had a fall the other day and had to go to hospital – so now poor Gareth is working on his own."

"So you won't have anyone exciting to play with," said Clare. "John's exciting, but he's going – he's a bad boy, isn't he, Mum? I'll tell you what he did, he did—"

"You are not to tell tales, Clare," said her mother. "Now just be quiet. You talk too much."

"I don't," said Clare. "I'm just being polite to visitors now. I'm just telling Nick and Katie that it's a pity they won't have anyone to play with. Except me, of course."

The children felt that they really didn't want to play with Clare – she would try to boss them, though they were both older than she was.

"We don't need anyone to play with," said Nick firmly. "We like being together and we'll find all sorts of things to do, especially as we're on holiday. You really needn't worry about us."

"Here we are," said Mrs Holly, turning into a long drive. "Holiday House! I hope you'll have a lovely time here and come back again often, especially later on in the summer holidays when we're packed out with children – it's fun then."

The drive curved round to a very big house – almost a mansion. At one end was a tall square tower, built in the same grey stone as the rest of the house. Ivy grew up the walls and surrounded most of the windows of the tower.

"I like it," said Katie. "It looks old and as if plenty of things have happened here."

"They have," said Mrs Holly, getting out of the car. "But we're quiet and peaceful now. Nothing tremendously exciting ever happens at Holiday House except things like picnics and parties. It's a house for children. Come along in."

Carrying their suitcases, the children went through the big, open double doors into a hall where the stone floor was set with bright rugs. Flowers stood about in tall vases and there was a scent of lilac as they walked down the hall. The children sniffed in pleasure – but not only at the smell of lilac! A delicious odour of baking cakes came from somewhere too.

"Mrs Potts is baking special scones," explained Clare. "That's because you've come. And she's made a fruitcake too, with cherries in. I saw it this morning."

This sounded good. The children felt very cheerful as they went up the big stone staircase on to a broad landing flooded with sunshine. Katie glanced out of one of the windows and exclaimed, "Oh, look, Nick, we're so near the sea!"

Nick went to the window and looked out too. Yes – the big house was almost on the beach, and the murmur of waves mingled with the seagulls' cries. It was good to see the sparkling sea, heaving and swelling so close to them.

"Your rooms look on to the sea, too," said Clare, reading his thoughts. "Mum, I'll take them to their rooms. I know which ones they are."

Clare seemed to know everything! Mrs Holly went downstairs while Clare led the way onwards, with the children and Punch behind. Nick slipped the terrier off the lead and he darted away to sniff in the corners.

Clare led them right down the corridor, and then off into a small, narrow passage with stone walls. It curved round after a bit and came out on to another landing, much narrower than the first one. From this a few little stone steps led up to a wooden door with an iron handle.

"Here's where you're sleeping," said Clare, and turned the handle. The door swung open and Katie gave a cry of pleasure. The big window opposite seemed full of sea and sky! They filled the room with a great clear light.

"This is really two rooms," said Clare, and pointed to a small door in the wall. "At least, it's one room, but Mum had it made into two. You each get a bit of the window – the other half of it is in this room here."

She opened the door in the wall, which was not made of stone, like the others, but of panelled wood, and the children looked through the doorway. Another room, just like the first one, was there.

"You take this inner room, Katie, and I'll have the other," said Nick, walking into the second room. "I say – isn't it great to be able to lean out of our window and look right down on the sea – it almost comes to the walls."

"If you hang out any further, Nick, you'll fall out – and it's a long way to the ground," called Katie.

Nick just laughed and swung back in with a piece of ivy in his hand.

"In winter we have to keep all these windows shut," said Clare, "because the waves splash into the rooms if we don't."

"Where's the tower?" asked Nick, going back into the first room. "I'd like to see that."

"Gareth has his room there," said Clare. "Gloomy Gareth! It's best to leave him alone. I think he's weird!" She went to the door and pointed to the end of the landing. "See that opening in the wall there? Well, that's where the spiral stairway begins. It goes all the way up to the tower. Gareth has the second room up. Nobody stays in the top one, because there's a crack in one wall and the roof is crumbling."

This all sounded very exciting. The children made up their minds to explore everywhere as soon as they could.

Nick was now getting rather tired of Clare, and thought it would be nice to be rid of her.

"We're going to unpack," he said. "You just show us the bathroom, Clare, and then you don't need to stay with us any longer."

"But I'd like to see you unpack," said Clare. "I don't mind staying."

Nick thought he had better put Clare in her place at once. "We'd rather unpack alone," he said firmly. "Now, where's the bathroom? Show us that and then scram."

Clare put on a scowl. "You might as well say straight out that you don't want me," she said.

"Too right – you've said it!" said Nick. "It's nice of you to help, but we can manage now. Where's the bathroom? It will soon be teatime and we really must wash."

"Find it yourself," said Clare rudely, and marched off. She slammed the door and then reopened it almost immediately.

"Tea's at five," she announced. "You'll hear a loud gong, and you'd better come quickly, or everything will be eaten."

The door slammed again. Nick gave a laugh. "Wow! Anyone would think she ran this place!"

"You weren't very nice to her," said Katie. "She'll probably tell her mother."

"Let her," said Nick. "Miss Rattle-Tongue will have to be kept in her place, Katie, or we'll never get rid of her."

Katie giggled. "What an awful name for her – but honestly she is a rattle-tongue. She goes on and on. She'll be nosy, too, I expect."

"Let's unpack," said Nick. "It's almost five o'clock. You go and find the bathroom, Katie, while I undo the cases."

"Right," said Katie, and went out of the door. She was soon back again. "It's near where the stairway goes up to the tower," she said. "It's a stone stairway, Nick – and it goes round and round as it goes up."

"We'll explore it later," said Nick. "Oh, no, there's the gong – it must be five o'clock. Quick, let's wash and go down – we'll unpack afterwards. Punch, where are you? Come along and have some tea!"

"And look out for Gruff, the cat!" said Katie. "The Cat-That-Can't-Be-Chased, Punch!"

CHAPTER 3

AT TEATIME

The children went out of the room with the little black-and-white terrier, down the corridor, through the narrow stone passage and out into the wider corridor whose windows overlooked the sea. They paused for a moment to gloat over the big stretch of brilliant blue sea, and then ran down the shallow steps of the great stone staircase.

Clare was waiting for them, of course! "I was just coming to fetch you," she said, "in case you lost your way."

She led them through a door and into a large, sunny room with many tables. A big one stood in the middle.

"This is the dining-room," said Clare. "Later in the summer, when we have lots of children, it's quite full. But now it seems very empty. You have to sit at this table here with Mum and me and Gareth and John."

The children sat down obediently, and Punch lay down at their feet. He was really a very well-behaved little dog. Nick looked round the room.

There were only three other people there – a woman dressed very neatly, a small girl sitting on a cushion on a chair at the table, and a baby in a high chair next to her.

The baby banged on the table with a spoon. It certainly was rather ugly, as Clare had said in the car, but it was a happy child and seldom cried. It was difficult to tell whether it was a boy or a girl, for its curly head and big mouth could quite well belong to either.

The small girl, Vicki, was a very dainty little thing, with fine golden curls fluffed up, and beautiful manners. Her nanny was cutting up jam sandwiches for her.

"She's spoilt!" said Clare, in a loud whisper. "She has everything she asks for. The baby's spoilt too. Fancy letting him bang that spoon without stopping!"

The nanny handed Vicki her plate of jam sandwiches. "Thank you, Nanny," said the little girl. Then she turned to look at the others. "I had an ice cream this afternoon," she said. "And I had a new boat. I'll show you."

"I've plenty of boats, thank you," said Clare. "I'm tired of seeing yours. You have something new every day. Why don't you stop that baby banging like that?"

"Take no notice of Clare," said the nanny to Vicki, who looked as if she was going to burst into tears. "There, there, darling – don't cry. You can show Mrs Holly your new boat after tea."

"Poor darling!" remarked Clare. "She's always a poor, dear darling. I wish you'd stop that baby banging his spoon."

"I shall complain to your mother about you again if you interfere," said the nanny crossly. "What with you and that boy John, there's no peace!"

The door flew open at that moment and a small boy about Clare's age came in. He grinned round at everybody and sat down at the table. "Can't we begin?" he said. "I heard the gong. Hello, Clare – where did you go in the car this afternoon?"

"Never you mind," said Clare. "This is Nick and this is Katie. I've told them you're going tomorrow."

"Yes, and it's because you kept sneaking on me," said John. He suddenly put on Clare's sharp-sounding voice, mimicking the way she spoke. "Oh, Mum, John climbed up to the top of the tower today, though you told him not to. Oh, Mum, John went swimming when the tide was in and you said he wasn't to. Oh, Mum, John went into the larder and took some tarts. Oh, Mum, he jumped out at me and hit me!"

The children laughed. John really did sound exactly like Clare. Clare flew into a temper and gave John a punch. He caught hold of her hands and held them tight.

"Naughty, naughty! Temper, temper! Apologise, Mummy's little tell-tale, or I won't let you go!"

The door opened again and in came two more people – Mrs Holly and a big dark-haired boy with a gloomy face. "Gloomy Gareth, of course," thought Katie. "Good, now perhaps we can have tea, and a bit of peace from Clare, too."

"Haven't you begun tea yet?" said Mrs Holly, in surprise. "I sent John to tell you not to wait for me."

"Well, he didn't come and tell us," said Clare. "He's only just arrived. Mum, tell him to let go of my hands."

"Apologise then, apologise, Mummy's little tell-tale, Mummy's little sneak!" said John.

"That's enough, John," said Mrs Holly. "Let Clare's hands go, or leave the table. I will not have this behaviour."

"Well, you won't have it much longer, Mrs Holly," said John, letting Clare's hands go. "I'm leaving tomorrow, hurray, hurray!"

"I can't imagine what our two new visitors will think of you," said Mrs Holly. She turned to the nanny at the table nearby. "And how is that darling baby, and dear little Vicki?" she asked.

"I've got a new boat," said Vicki. "I'll show it to you after tea."

"Thank you, darling," said Mrs Holly, and caught sight of a sudden scowl on Clare's face. She sighed. Why was Clare so difficult? Why wasn't she a bit more like that pretty, good-mannered Vicki? Really, she could be a very naughty little girl at times.

She caught sight of John putting jam and

cheese spread together on a slice of bread and butter. He grinned at her.

"You know you mustn't do that," she said. John popped the whole sandwich into his mouth at once. He gave it one bite and swallowed it.

"Sorry!" he said. "I had to eat it quickly in case you told me to give it to you. Shall I tell you all the bad things I've done today, before Clare tells you?"

"No," said Mrs Holly. "I'm really tired of you and your behaviour, John. I'm sorry to admit that I shall be very glad to say goodbye to you tomorrow – you'll be the first child I've ever felt like that about."

The tea was very, very good – there were the hot scones that the children had smelled as they entered the house, and big buttery slices of home-made bread, with jam, honey or peanut butter to go with them. There were little curranty rock-cakes that melted in your mouth, a big fruitcake, and a fat sponge sandwich with strawberry jam in the middle.

"I feel really hungry for the first time for weeks," said Katie, taking a scone.

"So do I," agreed Nick. "It's a brilliant

spread, Mrs Holly. I just hope I can manage to try everything!"

The children thoroughly enjoyed their tea. Mrs Holly smiled at them, glad to see two well-behaved children. She had had a truly dreadful time with John, who had made Clare even worse than usual – what a good thing he was going tomorrow!

"Would you like Clare to take you down to the beach after tea?" she asked the children. Nick shook his head at once, emptying his mouth quickly to answer.

"No, thank you, Mrs Holly," he said. "We've still got our things to unpack. We'll explore on our own when we've finished."

Katie had been watching the big boy, Gareth, eating his tea. Except for saying, "Hello, kids," in a rather surly voice when Mrs Holly told him their names, he hadn't said a single word.

"No wonder Clare calls him Gloomy Gareth!" Katie thought. "He looks as if he couldn't smile at all, and he's got a wrinkled forehead even though he's only fifteen. All the same, he has quite a nice face."

Mrs Holly chatted away through tea, talking to everyone, the nanny included.

She was a pleasant, cheerful person, not in the least like her sharp, bossy little daughter! She turned to the silent Gareth and asked him a question.

"Well, how did you get on with your work today, Gareth? All right, I hope?"

"Yes, thanks, Mrs Holly," said Gareth.

"Do you miss Mr Snell, your tutor?" asked Mrs Holly. "I hear he's getting on fairly well at the hospital. You'll be going to see him soon, I expect?"

"Yes, when I'm allowed to," said Gareth. "I do miss him – but I like being on my own."

"You're on your own too much," said Mrs Holly. "I don't like to see a boy alone as much as you are. Wouldn't you like to come for a picnic with us tomorrow?"

"I've too much work to do," said Gareth hurriedly. "Thank you all the same."

Tea was soon over – and nearly every plate and dish had been emptied, except for the one that held the big fruitcake. The children felt cheerful. If tea was like this, what would the other meals be like?

The nanny took Vicki and the baby out. "Come on, darling," she said to Vicki.

"We'll fetch your new boat and you can show it to kind Mrs Holly."

"But not to that horrid, disgusting girl Clare, dear, darling Vicki," said Clare under her breath.

Nick laughed. "What's wrong with Vicki?" he said to Clare. "She's a dear little girl!"

"Yuck!" said Clare rudely. "She's so spoilt she makes me want to scream."

"I suppose it's because you've had flu so badly and couldn't have your mother to yourself that you're so bad tempered, Clare," said Gareth unexpectedly. "You'll chase all your mother's guests away if you go on like this."

Mrs Holly had gone out of the room. Clare made a face at Gareth. "I don't like Mum having to take other children in," she said. "She hasn't enough time for me. All of you take her attention and I'm just nobody."

"Rubbish!" said Gareth. "You're so prickly that nobody wants you near them – that's the reason why we don't like you and why your mother can't get near you either!"

He stalked out of the room and went

upstairs. Clare's eyes suddenly filled with tears. She turned away and stamped her foot.

"He's so horrid to me!" she said fiercely. "He always is. So is everybody. And you two are going to be the same." She rushed out of the room and the children looked at one another in surprise.

"What a whirlwind!" said Nick. "Take no notice of her, Katie. We've got each other and we don't need to bother with Gloomy Gareth, or Rattle-Tongued Clare, or Dear, Darling Vicki!"

"And John will be gone tomorrow," said Katie. "Though I half wish he wasn't going. At least he's cheerful and lively! Come on, let's unpack, and then we'll explore."

CHAPTER 4

A LITTLE EXPLORING

The two children went up to their rooms and unpacked quickly. Katie put her clothes away neatly in the drawers of the oak chest there but Nick tipped everything out of his case on to the floor and then threw it all into his drawers.

"It's a tip in here already, Nick," said Katie, coming into Nick's room. "You'll never be able to find anything in that mess!"

It was lovely in the two rooms, with the glow of the sunlit sea lighting up the walls.

Nick bounced up and down on his bed. "At least it's really comfortable," he said. "I like this place, don't you, Katie?"

"Yes, I do," said Katie. "I wish we could have a swim this evening, but I don't expect we'd be allowed to, our first day."

She turned back to her own room, and Nick followed.

"Wow! Your room's neat," he said. "I don't know how you can live like this."

"We'll have to try and keep things neat," said Katie. "Mrs Holly doesn't seem to have much help in the house. I expect she does most things herself, and has more help in when the place is really crowded."

"Where's Punch?" said Nick, looking round. "Punch, come here! Punch!"

But no Punch came. "He must have slipped out of the door when I wasn't watching," Nick said. "It's my fault, I ought to have shut it. Punch! Punch!"

"He's probably gone after the Cat-That-Can't-Be-Chased," said Katie. "Let's go and find him."

Punch wasn't very far away. He was sniffing about in the corridor, near the spiral staircase up to the tower.

"Come along, Punch," said Katie. "We're going down to the beach. And let me tell you that it's no good hunting for rabbits there, because rabbits don't live on beaches!"

Halfway down the big staircase was a small landing, where the stairs turned at right angles. Punch bounded down the steps, and then stopped short at a very dark, solid black shadow in the corner of the little landing.

He growled. No sound came from the shadow. It merely sat still and waited.

Punch ran back a few steps and sniffed hard. "Cat!" he thought. "Yes, cat!" And at once he rushed at the black furry shadow in the corner to chase it.

The shadow didn't move – but when Punch came near enough it lifted a big paw and smacked him hard on the nose. Punch backed away at once.

Could this be a cat? Cats always ran when he came near. This one didn't. It just sat and waited to smack him. He barked, but the shadow still sat there. He ran at it again and – *biff!* He had an even harder smack that time. The little terrier backed away in such a hurry that he missed his footing and fell down the stairs. Over and over he rolled, and the big black cat came out of his corner and watched.

Bumpity-bumpity-bump! Punch was at the bottom, astonished and out of breath. He crept cautiously up a few steps, and the children, who had now come down to the landing, watched in amusement.

"Sssss!" said the cat warningly, as Punch crawled up yet another step. And then he spat extremely loudly, making even the children jump. Punch turned and ran down the stairs at top speed, and waited at the bottom for Nick and Katie.

They bent to stroke the big, thick-furred cat. "Well, Gruff, so you're the Cat-That-Can't-Be-Chased," said Nick with a laugh. "Punch, I hope you've learned that!"

Punch stayed cautiously at the bottom of the stairs. Gruff the cat came down solemnly and ponderously with the two children, purring like a kettle on the boil.

Punch backed away, but Gruff took not the slightest notice of him, and walked past with his nose in the air. Then, just as he had passed Punch, he turned and spat again very loudly indeed, and the terrier fled away in fright.

How the children laughed! "Punch will think twice before he chases another cat!" said Nick, scratching the big cat's ears. "Are you coming with us, Gruff? No? All right, we'll go and find Punch."

Punch joined them, tail between his legs,

as soon as they were out of doors. They explored the garden thoroughly, approving of the swings and the big seesaw. There was a large walled kitchen garden full of vegetables and fruit trees. A wooded, wilder part stretched beyond the wall, perfect for hide-and-seek. Finally, when they'd seen everything, they came back to the front and went through a little gate down to the beach.

The tide was high, but there was still a big piece of sandy beach to play on. "I expect the beach only gets completely covered at very high tides," said Nick. "Look, are those caves in the cliff over there, do you think?"

Katie looked to where Nick was pointing, some way along the beach, where the cliff rose high.

"Yes," she said, excited. "They are! We've always wanted to explore caves, Nick. Do you suppose smugglers ever came here at all?"

"They might have done," said Nick. "Mrs Holly would know. What's that place high up on the cliff, Katie? It looks rather like an old ruined house."

Katie gazed at it. "Yes – and it's very tumbledown. Look, the gulls are sitting on it now."

"That might be a good place to explore too," said Nick. "Let's ask Mrs Holly if we could have a picnic lunch one day, Katie, and go off on our own, exploring all round here."

"Oh, yes, let's," said Katie. "We'll get away from Clare then, won't we? Isn't she odd?"

"Well – more bad-tempered that odd," said Nick. "But she said Gareth was weird, and I did think he was a bit strange, didn't you?"

"Yes. Clare is about right when she calls him Gloomy Gareth!" said Katie, with a laugh. "I thought he looked sad too, Nick – as if he had a secret worry!"

"He probably has!" said Nick. "The kind of secret worry you get when you have to pass an exam and know that you haven't worked as hard as you should have done!"

"Oh, well – we're not likely to come up against him much," said Katie. "Let's paddle!"

So they paddled in the warm waves at

the edge of the sea. Then they picked up shells as pink as the sky at sunset – the sands were strewn with them when the tide began to go out.

"I like all these big rocks everywhere," said Katie, "and the rock pools. It's funny,

isn't it, that although Holiday House is built on the rocky cliff, when you're in the house and look out of the windows, it seems almost as if it's built right on the beach."

"Yes, but the cliffs are very low here," said Nick. "They rise up each side, so the house is sheltered in a dip. It looks great in the evening sun, doesn't it?"

It certainly did. The windows glinted and shone as if they were gold, and the tall tower rose up proud and high. The two children gazed at it.

"Clare said Gareth had the middle room," said Katie. "You can see the roof is falling away a bit here and there. What a pity not to mend it!"

"I don't suppose Mrs Holly's got enough money," said Nick. "She won't earn that much from taking in children."

"She works hard enough," said Katie. "Mum said she was a widow so I suppose she has to bring up Clare on her own."

"We'd better go back," said Nick, looking at his watch. "I hope we don't have to go to bed very early here, Katie. I wonder if we have supper."

"I hope so," said Katie. "I had an enormous tea, but I'm beginning to feel hungry again. I'd almost forgotten what it was like to feel hungry after being ill for so long. Where's Punch got to?"

Punch had been having a lovely time exploring the beach, sniffing at the bits of seaweed, scraping out shells with his paws, and chasing the waves when they ran down the beach. He backed away, barking, when they rolled up again.

"He doesn't like getting his feet wet!" said Katie, with a laugh. "He thinks he's going to have a bath!"

A voice hailed them. "Oh, there you are! I've been looking for you everywhere. You're to come in now."

It was Clare, of course! She was standing at the gate, a sturdy little figure, very determined-looking.

"Who said we were to come in?" demanded Nick.

"My mother did," said Clare. "And she asked if you wanted supper, because you can have some if you like, but not if you don't want to."

"Well, we do want to," said Nick,

climbing up to the gate. "Are you going to have some, Clare?"

"Of course. I always do," said Clare. "It's tuna salad tonight, and red jelly. Hurry!"

They ran up the beach at once. Tuna salad sounded nice, so did the jelly. "You've got to wash first," said Clare, in her bossiest voice.

Someone nearby repeated this, mimicking Clare's voice exactly. "You've got to wash first, you've got to wash first!"

It was John watching from a corner of the garden. "And don't forget to cut your nails and polish your ears and shine up your toes!" he chanted, still in Clare's voice. She charged at him furiously but he ran to a window, climbed in and disappeared. He was sitting demurely at the table with Gareth when the others went in. Clare gave him a scowl.

He gave her one back, making such a startling face that the children stared at him, fascinated. He obligingly made a few more. Then Mrs Holly came in and he gazed at her with the most innocent expression. The children thought he was a very surprising person and felt quite sorry that he was leaving Holiday House.

Punch settled down under the table. Gruff the cat arrived and saw Punch there. He advanced majestically to the table, and Punch fled to a corner of the fireplace! Gruff sat down on the very spot under the table where Punch had been lying, purring loudly.

"Ah," said Clare, in a pleased voice. "Gruff has already taught Punch his manners, I see. Good old Gruff!"

"Tuna salad?" said Mrs Holly to the children, and they held out their plates.

"We saw the caves in the cliffs from the beach," said Nick. "Were there ever smugglers near Tolly Sands?"

"Oh, yes, lots," answered Clare. "At Tolly House, that old ruined place up on the cliff, they used to shine a light out to sea to tell the smugglers that it was safe to sail into the bay."

"What about Holiday House?" asked Katie. "It's very old as well."

"I expect the people living here must have known about the smugglers," said Mrs Holly. "We haven't lived here very long so we don't know much about its history."

"There are lots of old books in the library," said Gareth unexpectedly. "You could look in some of those and see if you can find anything about smugglers around this coast."

Katie gave a sudden yawn. Mrs Holly smiled. "Ah, you're tired! I thought you would be, you've had a long day. Bed for you two immediately after supper!"

"I'm going to stay up late tonight," announced John. "It's my last night."

"You may stay up till half-past eight, and no later," said Mrs Holly.

"What time does Gareth go to bed?" inquired Katie. "Any time he likes?"

"Well, he's old enough to be sensible and choose his own bedtime," said Mrs Holly. "Now, have you finished? Off to bed then, and sleep well!"

The children went off together, Nick yawning as well now.

"See you tomorrow, Katie," he said, as she went into the inner bedroom. "We're going to have a lovely time here!"

CHAPTER 5

UP IN THE TOWER

It really was fun at Holiday House. The children soon settled down and enjoyed everything. The food was splendid, and after only a few days they began to look much healthier after their long weeks of illness.

John, the naughty boy, had left. The nanny and Vicki and the baby were still there, but mixed very rarely with the others. Gareth appeared only at meal-times, looking as gloomy as ever. His tutor was still in hospital, so he was working by himself.

"Doesn't Gareth every play or swim or do anything but work, Mrs Holly?" asked Nick one day at teatime. "I wouldn't have thought that his parents would want him to work so hard. He looks really tired sometimes."

"He hasn't any parents," said Mrs Holly.

"Only an uncle who is very stern with him. His uncle's shut up his house and gone off somewhere on business, and that's why Gareth is here."

"Hasn't he any brothers or sisters?" said Katie.

"He's got a brother," said Clare, unexpectedly.

"I don't think he has, Clare," said her mother. "He's never said anything about one."

"Well, the woman at the sweet shop told me," said Clare. "And when I asked where he was she wouldn't tell me. There's a mystery about the brother, I think."

"Oh, don't be silly, Clare," said her mother impatiently. "And I wish you wouldn't go and gossip in the village like that."

"I like gossip," said Clare. "I've heard all sorts of strange things since I've been here, Mum. I heard something funny about James, the gardener. He—"

"Leave the table, Clare," said her mother.

"Well, I won't tell you if you don't want to hear, but it's very funny," said Clare, not leaving the table.

"LEAVE THE TABLE," said Mrs Holly. Clare stared obstinately at her mother. The door opened at that moment and in came Gareth.

"Sorry I'm late, Mrs Holly," he said briefly. Clare handed him the scones, not looking at her mother.

"Gareth, would you mind removing Clare for me?" said Mrs Holly. "She has misbehaved and I have told her to leave the table."

"Don't you dare touch me!" cried Clare, and shot out of her chair at top speed. The door banged, and steps could be heard running down the hall.

"Dear, dear – I shall be glad when Clare goes back to school and has a bit of discipline," said Mrs Holly. "Katie, have some cake, dear?"

Gareth sat silently at the table, looking so forlorn that Mrs Holly felt worried about him.

"Gareth, you really are working too hard," she said. "You mustn't do any work this evening. Go down to the beach and have a nice long walk. I insist!"

"All right, Mrs Holly, I will," said

Gareth, giving her a small smile that vanished almost at once. And immediately after tea the children saw him going out into the garden and disappearing through the little beach-gate.

"Well, I do hope he has a nice long walk," said Mrs Holly. "I never knew such a lonely boy. He never gets a letter, he never seems to stop working and he's alone in that tower-room of his for hours and hours on end!"

"Oh, Mrs Holly, that reminds me – do you think we might go up to the tower this evening?" asked Nick. "You said we might, if we were careful, but we haven't been yet."

"Yes, you may," said Mrs Holly, feeling thankful for the hundredth time that these children were pleasant and trustworthy. She so often had ones that weren't! "I'll give you the key to the tower-room – it's falling to pieces, you know, so I have to keep the door to it locked in case silly children like John go exploring."

She took a large key from her desk and gave it to Nick. "Here you are. Lock the door behind you when you come down and bring me back the key."

The children went off upstairs. "There ought to be a wonderful view from the top of the tower!" said Katie. "Oh, bother, here's Clare! Pretend we're going to have a game in our rooms!"

"What shall we play?" said Nick at once. "Snap or draughts?"

"Draughts," said Katie, afraid of saying snap in case Clare decided to join in.

"If you play snap I'll play, too," said Clare, coming up and patting Punch, who was with them.

"We're not going to play snap," said Nick.

"You don't want me!" said Clare. "Nor does Mummy. She sent me away from the table and I didn't finish my tea. All the same, I did hear that Gareth had a brother."

"Well, ask him if he has, if you're so interested!" said Nick. "I've never met such an inquisitive person, Clare – always interfering and bossing people!"

"The only person that really likes me is Gruff the cat," Clare said mournfully.

"Well, I'm not surprised. You're very alike – both inquisitive and both bossy!" said Nick. "Gruff biffs Punch on the nose whenever he goes past him, and I always feel that you'd like to biff people you don't like, too."

"I thought you were nice at first but you aren't," said Clare, turning away. "I wish I was back at school. I can run lots of things there without being told I'm bossy."

She ran off down the stairs, and the children went into their bedrooms. Nick looked out of the window and then called Katie.

"Look – isn't that Gareth slouching along the beach? He's going towards that old tumbledown house up on the cliffs."

"Yes, it *is* Gareth," said Katie. "He's staring and staring at the house now. Isn't he odd, Nick? Stands and looks for ages at an old house, and yet never notices the sunset on the sea or the gulls soaring over his head!"

"I suppose he's working too hard," said Nick. "Come on, Katie. Let's see if that inquisitive little Clare is hanging about. If not, we'll go up the tower. Stay here, Punch."

They looked out of Nick's bedroom door. No one seemed to be about at all, not even

Gruff the cat. They made their way down the corridor to the staircase that spiralled up the tower.

They climbed up holding on to the rail, because the inner side of the stone stairs was very narrow. They came to a small stone landing, and saw a door standing open there – a stout wooden door, studded with great nails.

They looked inside. It was the first room in the tower, and was used for junk. Boxes, trunks, old unwanted crates were there, as well as extra chairs and tables used in the summer when Holiday House was full of guests. It was so packed with stuff that the two children could hardly move inside. They came out and went up the stone stairway once more. It wound round and round, and arrived at a second stone landing, where there was a similar door to the one below. But this one was shut.

"Shall we open it and peep inside?" said Nick. "I'd like to see Gareth's room."

They opened it. It was a bed-sitting room, untidy and full of papers and books. Evidently Gareth was very hard at work! The table was piled high with reference books and paper that was scribbled on in small handwriting. The window overlooked the sea, and the room was very light in the evening sun.

They didn't go inside but shut the door quietly. Then they went on again up the spiral staircase, and came to a third room. The door to this was locked. Nick took the key from his pocket and slid it into the lock. The door opened and the two children went in.

Part of the roof had fallen in, and the window was broken. It looked very desolate, this top room of the tower – but, oh, the view! The children stood and gazed at it. The window looked out over miles of sea, which the sinking sun turned golden.

They could see the old house over on the cliff quite easily – in fact the tower they were in was so high that they almost looked down on the house. Nick suddenly pointed to it.

"Look, Katie – isn't that someone standing at the window of the old house? See, towards the top."

Katie looked hard. "Yes," she said at last. "It is someone. Let's wave."

"No, don't," said Nick. "It could be Gareth and he might think we've come into the tower to snoop round his room or something. Oh, look – he's gone."

They stood in the tower for a little longer and then left. Nick locked the door behind him and the two children went down the spiral stairs, holding on to the rail.

"Well, that was quite exciting," said Katie. "I wish we had Gareth's room. It would be fun to sleep in a tower like this."

They went down to the swings in the garden and swung to and fro, enjoying the swift flight through the air and back. Mrs Holly came out and called to them after a while, "Well, did you see the tower?"

"Yes!" called back Nick. "There's a brilliant view from the top. I wish we had our room there!"

"Did you bring me back the key?" asked Mrs Holly.

"Oh, no! I locked the door but I must have left the key in the lock!" said Nick, embarrassed. He leaped off the swing. "I'll go and get it straight away, Mrs Holly. I'm so sorry."

He ran into the house and upstairs, along the corridors, and came to the spiral staircase set in the wall. He ran up it lightly, slowing down as he came to the top, for the steps were very steep. Yes, there was the great key in the lock!

Nick was just about to take it out when he stopped. He heard a noise in the locked tower-room! He stood and listened. Yes, there was the noise again – the scrape of someone's feet on the stone floor! The someone cleared his throat and then there was the sound of a yawn!

But – the tower-room was locked! Nick tried the door softly. Yes, he had locked it when he and Katie came out. And yet, there was someone in there! Who was it? And how had that someone entered when the door had been well and truly locked?

He took the key silently out of the lock and ran down the spiral stairs. He must tell Katie! This was very odd indeed.

CHAPTER 6

CLARE GETS INTO TROUBLE

Nick went out to the garden to find Katie. Mrs Holly was there, talking to his sister. He gave her the key, and she took it indoors with her.

"Katie, come somewhere private," said Nick, in a low voice. "I've got something very strange to tell you."

Katie was astonished. She slipped off the swing at once. "Where shall we go?" she said. "Our bedrooms, I think, don't you?"

So they went to Nick's bedroom, keeping a sharp eye out for Clare. Punch ran with them, sensing their excitement, panting a little as he went, his tail wagging hard.

The children shut the door of Nick's room. "Now, what is it?" said Katie.

"Listen. You saw me lock the top tower-room, didn't you?" said Nick, whispering still.

Katie nodded.

"Well," went on Nick, "I left the key in the lock after locking the door – but, Katie, when I went to get the key just a few minutes ago, I heard somebody in the room behind the door!"

Katie stared at him. "You couldn't have!" she said. "There was no one in there when we left and locked the door. No one at all."

"Well, there is now, unless he's gone," said Nick. "Let's go and see. But don't make a sound!"

They left Punch behind and went quietly out of the room, down the corridor and up the spiral stairs. When they came to Gareth's room, they heard him whistling softly, as he sometimes did, and the sound of a book being dropped on to the floor.

"He must have just come back," said Nick, in a whisper. "Don't let him hear us."

They went on up the stairs to the top room. They stood outside it, listening.

There was no sound at all this time. Not a scrape of a foot, not a yawn. They stood there for some time and then looked at one another.

"Peep through the keyhole," said Katie, in Nick's ear. So he bent down and looked.

The keyhole was large and gave a good view of the room. But it was empty – at least, all the part he could see was perfectly empty!

They went down the stairs softly, puzzled. "Somebody was in that locked room – and now he's not," said Nick. "Who was it? And how did he get through a door, both in and out, when it was locked? It's a mystery!"

Clare met them at the bottom of the spiral stairway. "I've been looking for you," she said. "Where have you been? Gareth won't be very pleased if you keep popping in to see him when he's at work."

"We haven't been to see him," said Katie, before she could stop herself.

"Oh! Then have you been up to the top tower-room?" said the inquisitive Clare. "You can't get in. It's locked. I can get you the key though. I know where it is."

"We can get it from your mother, thank you, if we want it," said Nick. "Er – do you often go up there, Clare?"

"Never," said Clare. "I did at first, but I soon got tired of it. There's nothing to see up there except miles of sea. Please come and have a game with me. I feel lonely."

"All right," said Nick, thinking that Clare looked rather sad. He remembered that she had had hardly any tea, and he took her into his room, with Katie tagging behind, looking rather cross because she badly wanted to talk to Nick about the strange puzzle of the top tower-room.

"Have some chocolate?" said kind-hearted Nick, handing a bar to Clare. She took it at once.

"Thanks," she said. "I do think Mum was mean, don't you? Sending me away from the table like that just because I said I'd heard something about James."

"I don't think your mother's mean," said Nick. "I like her."

"She likes you and Katie too," said Clare, munching away hard. "She says you've got good manners, and you're trustworthy. When she told me I was sure she meant that I wasn't good-mannered and that I'm not trustworthy."

"Of course she didn't," said Katie, irritated. "She's too nice to say mean things like that."

"Don't you sometimes think your mother's mean?" asked Clare, finishing the last of the chocolate and licking her fingers.

"No way! We love her," said Katie, shocked. "And anyway, if we ever did think she'd been mean we wouldn't say it to other people, like you do about your mother. We'd think that was disloyal."

"Oh well, we're different, I suppose," said Clare. "Did you see Gareth when you went up the tower? Is he back from his walk?"

"Yes," said Nick. "We heard him in his room."

"You know, it's true that he's got a brother," said Clare, speaking in a half whisper. "And it's true, there's some mystery about him. I think he's in prison or something. Anyway, the woman at the sweet shop says she heard he was a bad lot, a very bad lot."

"I think you're horrible to go listening to tales like that, when you know they may be lies," said Nick, disgusted. "I don't believe there's a word of truth in it. Why do you have to go snooping around, listening to gossip about people?"

"Well, it interests me," said Clare. "I like hearing things about people."

"Especially nasty things, I suppose," said Katie scornfully.

Clare got up and brushed some chocolate crumbs off her dress. She stared angrily at Katie. "I don't know why you speak to me in that nasty way," she said. "Do you know what I'm going to do? I'm going to ask Gareth if he's got a brother. I shall ask him straight out!"

She marched out of the room, and the children made little faces at one another. "I don't like her," said Nick. "It's a good thing you and I have no secrets, or anything we don't want people to know about, Katie. Clare would ferret it out in no time! Do you think she really will ask Gareth about his brother?"

"Yes. She's bold enough for anything," said Katie, getting out some cards. "But I don't expect this brother business will come to anything! It's just Clare's nastiness – she makes people tell her silly tales. I've a good mind to tell her a few myself!"

"Great idea! Let's!" said Nick, laughing.

"I'll tell her we've got an uncle who the police are after, and you tell her we've got a cousin who – who—"

"Who lets his horse sleep with him in his bedroom," said Katie, with a giggle, remembering a silly story she'd once read.

Nick remembered the mystery of the top tower, and put down his cards. "About that tower-room," he said, lowering his voice. "We really must find out how somebody got in there when the door was locked – and how he disappeared again while the door was still locked. Shall we tell Mrs Holly?"

Katie looked thoughtful. "No," she said. "It sounds a bit silly, and I don't think she'd believe you. She'd probably think it was Gareth who had gone up there for something. Or she'd say you hadn't locked the door."

"All right. We'll keep it to ourselves," said Nick, dealing the cards. "What do you say, Punch-dog? Shall we keep it a secret? We ought to have taken you up to the tower-room with us to have a good sniff round!"

Punch cocked his ears and listened. He loved being talked to. He put a paw on Nick's knee as if to say, "Go on – I'm listening."

Then, quite suddenly, he ran to the door

and barked loudly, pawing at it. The children looked at him in surprise.

"What can he hear?" said Nick – and then he and Katie heard something too!

They heard a noise of squealing, and of bumping and clattering – and then sobbing. What on earth could have happened?

Nick flung open the door and ran out, followed by Katie and Punch. Punch raced down the corridor to the spiral staircase at the end. Sitting on the bottom step, howling, was Clare. She was rubbing her right leg as if it hurt her.

A voice came down the stairs. "Howl all you like, you little pest, but don't you dare come interrupting me again when I'm working!" Then a door slammed loudly.

"What happened?" said Nick. "Are you hurt?"

"Yes," sobbed Clare. "I think my leg is broken, or something. That horrible Gareth!"

"Your leg's not broken," said Nick, and he helped Clare up. "Come to our rooms and we'll have a look at it. It's only a graze. It serves you right, Clare – you shouldn't have gone pestering Gareth."

Clare limped to the children's rooms and sank down on Nick's bed. She rubbed the tears from her eyes.

"Gareth's a beast," she said. "All I did was to go into his room – and I knocked on his door first for politeness, and I said, I said . . ." She stopped and gave a little sob. "All I said was, 'Oh, Gareth, I've heard you have a brother. Is it true?' And he stared at me in a most horrible way – stared and stared – and he said, he said . . ."

"Well, what did he say?" said Katie impatiently.

"He suddenly shouted at me," said Clare. "He shouted, 'What do you mean, have I got a brother? NO, I HAVEN'T, so clear out of here!' And he got up and ran at me, and I was frightened and rushed out of the door . . ."

"And fell down the spiral stairway, I suppose?" said Nick. "Well, now you know that the tale you heard was untrue, and I hope you're satisfied! And I advise you not to go and tell tales to your mother, or she may shout at you, too. Here, bind up your knee with this hanky, and stop howling."

Clare dried her eyes and looked obstinate. She began to tie up her knee. "All right," she said. "Say what you like but I think Gareth's a fibber. I bet he's got a brother, no matter what he says!"

And how surprised she was to find the children suddenly pushing her out of their room in disgust, and pushing her so hard that she fell down the few steps that led up to their rooms! Poor Clare, she really did make trouble for herself, and this time there was nobody to help her!

CHAPTER 7

THE PICNIC

The next week a few more children came to stay at Holiday House, but they were mostly very young, all under four years old, too young for either Clare or the children to play with. "Dear, darling Vicki" and her baby brother were still there, with their fussy nanny, who lost no chance of ticking off Clare if she could.

And Clare in her turn lost no chance of making loud remarks about Vicki and the baby. She really was a very difficult girl, the children decided. Vicki was a good little thing and Katie thought that the baby boy was fun to watch, crawling over the beach in his tiny pair of shorts.

"Do you notice that if Mrs Holly makes a real fuss of any child, Clare is sure to have her knife into him or her, and can't find a good thing to say about them?" said Katie one day.

"Yes – and have you seen her face when her mother makes a fuss of Vicki?" asked Nick. "I think she's jealous. I wish some children of her own age would come along, so that she could play with them – I get tired of her tagging along after us."

"I'm getting a couple of helpers in," said Mrs Holly one evening, a few days after Clare's quarrel with Gareth. "Mrs Potts is going to need somebody to help her in the kitchen, and I shall need someone else to help with the bedrooms."

"Who are you getting, Mum?" asked Clare at once. "Anyone from near here?"

"Yes, dear, Mrs Tomms, from the village, to help Mrs Potts, and Lydia Jordans to help with the rooms," said her mother. "She came to see me yesterday – she's pretty and rather shy and she comes from Tiddington, not from our village. I liked her very much."

Clare, of course, went to have a good look at Mrs Tomms as soon as she arrived. Mrs Tomms was tall and stout and red-faced. She also had a very loud voice, and made it quite clear to Clare that she was not going to have children in her kitchen!

"It's Mrs Potts's kitchen, not yours," said Clare indignantly, and went over to the fridge to see if Mrs Potts had made a nice pudding for supper.

But she found Mrs Tomms standing in front of the fridge door. "Aha! So you're after the fridge, are you?" she said. "Off you go, missy – and don't let me see you here again, or I'll report you to Mrs Holly."

"That wouldn't be any good," Clare said jeeringly. "She's my mother."

"Mother or not, I'll go to her the first time you come near the fridge!" said Mrs Tomms in her loud voice, and Clare decided that it would really be best to turn her back and go! She went off to find Lydia Jordans, who was making beds.

Clare stood in the doorway and looked at her. She was certainly a pretty, slim girl, with soft, golden hair round her face, and shy eyes that looked down at the floor when she spoke. Her voice was very soft too, quite the opposite of Mrs Tomm's loud bark.

"Hello," said Clare. "I'm Clare Holly, Mrs Holly's daughter. You're Lydia Jordans, aren't you?"

"Yes," said Lydia, in her soft voice.

"You come from Tiddington, don't you?" asked Clare, and began to ply the soft-voiced, deft-handed Lydia with questions as she moved round the room, dusting.

Lydia answered politely but shyly. Clare heard her mother calling her and went off, pleased with Lydia. She would make friends with her, and perhaps get her to give her something out of the fridge, now that she was afraid to go into the kitchen with that horrid Mrs Tomms there.

Mrs Holly wanted Clare to help to get ready a picnic lunch. "I just feel as if I must get away from the house for a few hours," she said to Clare. "I've been working too hard, I think. You help to get the picnic basket ready, Clare, and we'll take the children and Gareth with us. We'll go and have a picnic in that nice cove just below the old house on the cliff."

"All right, Mum," said Clare. "You have been working too hard. You deserve a nice picnic. But don't let's ask Gareth. He's so gloomy, he'll spoil everything."

"I want him to come," said Mrs Holly. "He's another one that works very hard. Go and tell Katie, Nick and Gareth about the picnic. They can all go in swimsuits if they take towels and jerseys too."

Clare went to tell them – at least, she told Katie and Nick and asked them to tell Gareth. She hadn't said a single word to the big boy ever since the time she had fallen down the spiral stairs – but as Gareth had never spoken much to her, nobody really noticed this except Nick and Katie.

They all set off for the picnic, Punch too, walking over the warm sand to the little cove beneath the cliff where the old house stood. This cove could only be reached when the tide was out, because the sea came right up to the cliffs when it was high, and beat against them tumultuously.

"One day," said Mrs Holly, looking up at the old house, "one day there'll be a tremendous storm, and the old place will fall into the sea! Then this little cove will disappear under bricks and stone and rubble."

"Oh, Mum – you don't think it will begin to fall yet, do you?" asked Clare in alarm, looking up at the old house, which did seem to lean a little over the cliff!

Her mother laughed.

"No. Don't be afraid," she said, "it's been like that for years. The owners left it because they were told that it was dangerous to live in – but it might well stay up there until the next century. The roof is going now, and the old place will soon be a complete ruin. Pass the basket, Clare dear. I expect you're all starving."

They were, of course – even Gareth, who didn't usually have much appetite. The gulls flew down nearby and gobbled the bits that the children threw to them. The sea sent tiny, lace-edged waves up the smooth golden sand, and there was a continual lapping noise round the nearby rocks, very pleasant to hear.

"I do love Tolly Sands," said Katie, leaning back to feel the sun on her face. "It's such a peaceful place. Another sandwich, please, Nick."

"Who made these sandwiches?" asked Nick. "I've never tasted such nice ones before! What's in them?"

"Ask Mrs Tomms!" said Mrs Holly. "She made them. I think she's going to be a great help in the kitchen."

"I don't like her," said Clare. "She doesn't talk, she shouts. I like Lydia, though."

"Who's Lydia?" asked Nick, who hadn't yet seen her.

"Her name is Lydia Jordans," began Clare, who always enjoyed giving information about anyone, "and she comes from—"

Gareth suddenly interrupted her. He had been lying on his back, eating sandwiches. Now he sat up and looked at Clare.

"What name did you say?" he said, sounding very interested.

"I said, Lydia Jordans," answered Clare, "and she comes from Tiddington. She's got a brother who's been away at work, but he's come back now, and a big sister and a little sister, and she likes needlework and going for long walks and dogs and cats and—"

"Really! Need we have all these details about Lydia?" said Mrs Holly. "I don't know how you manage to get them, Clare. I wish you wouldn't talk to people the way you do, finding out this, that and the other. They don't like it – they think you're prying into their affairs."

Gareth was still looking at Clare, and the children stared at him in surprise. He didn't usually listen to anything that Clare said. "Are you sure her name's Lydia Jordans?" he asked.

"Yes," said Clare, surprised.

"Did she tell you the names of her brother and sisters?" asked Gareth, in such a strange voice that everyone stared at him.

"Yes. Her big sister's name is Rachel and her little sister's name is Louise, and her brother's name is Sam," said Clare promptly. "Louise goes to school, Rachel is married and she's got a baby called Jake, and Sam has just come back from Scotland, where he's been working with his uncle. He's got a job in a bicycle shop, Lydia says."

"Clare! *Must* you ask people about their intimate family affairs like this?" said her mother in horror. "Really, you'll be telling us next that her father's got corns and the mother's got—"

"Oh, he has got corns," said Clare, sounding surprised. "That was a good guess of yours, Mum. He has to go and have them—"

"That's enough, Clare, that's really enough," said Mrs Holly with a groan. "I can't bear any more. Gareth – where are you going?"

Gareth had got up suddenly, taken his jersey from the sand, and was walking away over the beach. He hadn't said a word of farewell, and everyone looked after him in astonishment.

"Gareth!" called Mrs Holly. "I'm speaking to you! Where are you going? We haven't finished the picnic yet – there's still plenty to eat."

Gareth turned, and the children saw that he looked upset.

"I'm going back to the house," he muttered. "I – I just don't feel well. Touch of the sun, perhaps. Don't worry about me, please." He went slowly over the beach, and the rest of the picnic party looked at one another, puzzled.

"Gloomy Gareth!" said Clare. "I told you I didn't want him, Mum. He always spoils everything."

"But he was quite all right until you began to go on and on about Lydia and her family," said Nick. "He was enjoying himself, and eating away just like we all were."

"Well, he can't have been upset by Clare's silly string of facts about Lydia," said Mrs Holly. "Really, Clare, we didn't need to know the names of the sisters and brother and all they were doing – you ought to be ashamed of yourself."

After that, the picnic was quite spoilt. Mrs Holly went back to Holiday House with the basket, Clare wandered off to collect shells and the children lay on their backs and looked up at the old house leaning above them on the cliff.

"Let's go and explore it," said Nick. "Come on, Katie – we've always wanted to. Get up, lazy-bones, or I'll leave you behind and go by myself."

CHAPTER 8

A Most Exciting Discovery

The children made their way up a little
path towards the old house. Like Holiday
House it was built of stone, and was very
solid-looking indeed.

Punch ran along in front of the two
children. He had enjoyed the picnic very
much, having had a large number of titbits
from everyone. No one could help loving
the lively black-and-white dog with his
pointed nose and short waggy tail.

The path was very crumbly, and the
children had to go carefully. They reached
the top of the cliff at last and stood still in
what once must have been part of the
garden to get their breath back, looking at
the old house.

"Half of the garden has tumbled over the
cliff into the sea at some time," said Nick.
"Look where this wall is broken in half,
right at the edge."

The house looked sad and deserted and the guttering hung down here and there. The children went over to the back door, which turned out to be locked. The windows were all tightly fastened, though most of the panes were cracked. Nick and Katie went round to the other side of the house. The front door was locked too.

"I wonder how Gareth got into the house," said Nick, puzzled. "That is, if it was Gareth we saw in here the other day, standing at one of the top windows."

"Well, if it wasn't Gareth, it must have been somebody else – possibly a tramp," said Katie. "Somebody got in somewhere – but where?"

They went all round the house, but there was no sign of anyone getting in anywhere. They knew that it would have been dangerous to climb in through one of the broken windows, because the glass was sharp and jagged.

There seemed to be absolutely no way of getting into the house at all, much to the children's surprise. How had Gareth got in then – if it had been Gareth?

"No footmarks anywhere in the sand

around the house," said Nick. "Not a sign to show that anyone has ever been here!"

"We could ask Gareth how he got in," said Katie. She was puzzled too. "And if it wasn't him, we'll tell Mrs Holly that somebody's prowling about!"

"It's rather disappointing," said Nick. "I was looking forward to a spot of exploring."

"I know!" said Katie. "Let's go and explore a cave or two. We've never been into any except that first little one with Clare, because we've never had our torches with us."

"We haven't got them now," said Nick.

"I know – but we can easily go and get them," said Katie. "I'll run back to the house and find them. You stay here, I won't be a minute. I'll take Punch and shut him into our room – he wouldn't like dark caves."

She ran off over the beach at top speed, Punch racing with her. In fifteen minutes she was back with the torches, and the children began to climb up to the caves that lay like black shadows here and there in the cliffs.

They were very disappointing caves,

shallow and low-roofed. The first one was so small that the children couldn't stand upright in it. The next one went back a little way and had a higher roof, but it smelled of rotting seaweed and they soon came out.

"I don't think much of these caves," said Nick. "No wonder nobody ever bothers to go and picnic in them or explore them. There's nothing to explore."

"Let's go and have a swim," said Katie. "I'm bored with caves now."

"We'll just try one last one," said Nick, and climbed up to it, his torch stuck in his belt, for he needed both hands.

He found himself on a rocky ledge outside the cave. It had a very low roof in front, and the children had to bend almost double to make their way in, but inside it was much higher, and the cave broadened out well. In fact, it was the biggest one they had seen.

"This one's a fantastic cave!" said Nick in surprise. "It goes really far back. Come on, Katie, let's see how big it is."

The cave was almost dark, for very little daylight came in at the low entrance. Their

82

torches showed them a very spacious place indeed, and not at all smelly as some of the caves had been. They walked right to the back of it.

"This would make a wonderful place for a hidy-hole," said Nick, flashing his torch round. Then suddenly he kept his torch pointing steadily at one place – right in the very corner of the cave.

"Look, Katie!" he exclaimed.

Katie looked at the spot lit by Nick's bright torch. "What's that?" she said. "It's a hole, isn't it? A hole in the rocky floor!"

They both bent over and looked at the hole. "Does it lead anywhere, do you think?" asked Katie. "It's not big enough for us to get into."

"It might be," said Nick, kicking away sand and old seaweed from the hole. "It's partly stuffed up with all kinds of things – sand, seaweed and, look, this bit of loose rock has fallen in from the cave-wall, and blocked it too. Help me to lift it, Katie!"

He and Katie tugged hard at the rock which lay partly across the hole. They dragged it away at last and then cleared out more seaweed and sand. Nick shone his torch into the hole, and saw that it went down some way.

"I can't see if it goes down to another cave, or whether it has a rocky bottom to it," he said, red with excitement. "I know – take my torch, Katie, and I'll let myself carefully down into the hole and see what happens. If I touch rock with my feet I'll know it's just a hole. If I don't, I shall know it's a way through to somewhere else – another cave, perhaps!"

Katie watched him, half frightened. He let himself down – but there was no rocky bottom to rest his feet on! Instead, the hole seemed to widen out tremendously. "I'm going to get out again," he said. "Then I want you to hold my feet, Katie, while I lean down into the hole as far as I can with my torch. I think there may be another cave underneath – perhaps one that nobody has ever been in!"

"Oh, please be careful!" said Katie anxiously. She helped Nick out of the hole, and he lay down full length, his shoulders and head right in the hole. He held his torch out at arm's length down the dark hole, while Katie hung on to his feet.

He gave a shout. "It does go into another cave! I can see the rocky floor below. We can easily let ourselves drop down on to the sand!"

Katie pulled him back, and he got into the hole feet first again. There were ledges he could put his feet on as he went down,

and then he let himself drop the last few metres on to soft sand below. He was out of the hole! He shone his torch round and called excitedly up to his sister.

"Katie, it's not another cave – it's a tunnel, a kind of underground passage. Come down too – it's quite easy!"

Katie got into the hole, her heart beating fast. This really was an adventure! She cautiously felt about with her feet, and let herself down gently.

"Now let yourself go," called Nick. "Then you'll drop on to the sand like I did."

Katie let herself go, and fell to the soft sand below. Nick caught and steadied her. She looked round in wonder.

"You're not frightened, are you, Katie?" asked Nick. "Isn't this exciting? Who would have thought that the cave above had a hole that led to this passage!"

They stood side by side in the darkness. The roof was only just above their heads, and they could touch the sides when they held their hands a little way out.

Nick shone his torch first up, then down, the passage. "Where does it come from?" he wondered. "And where does it lead to? Katie, which way shall we take? This way leads in the direction of Holiday House, and this way leads in the opposite direction."

"Let's take this way, the opposite direction!" said Katie. "I don't care which! We can easily explore both ways if we want to! You lead, Nick."

So Nick led the way, his torch making a bright pathway of golden light in front of them, showing up the passage as it twisted and turned deep down in the cliff. Once the roof became so low that Nick halted, afraid that he could go no further. But just beyond, the low part of the roof rose again, and the two went on and on.

Suddenly, Nick stopped once more and gave an astonished shout. "Hello! What's this? Steps, Katie – steps leading upwards, look!"

Katie pressed close to him and looked over his shoulder. There were steps there, hewn out of the brown rock many years ago! They were rough and badly shaped, but they were certainly steps!

"Go on, Nick, climb the steps!" said

Katie in excitement. "Where do they lead to?"

Nick went up slowly. The worn, rough-hewn steps told him that other people had used this passage – many, many others, in days gone by. He and Katie were not the first ones to walk along this twisty tunnel in the cliffs, as he had imagined.

There were eleven steps, steep and rough. At the top was a doorway. Not a door, but a doorway. The door itself lay just inside, broken from its hinges, old and rotten!

Nick gave it a kick and some of it fell to pieces. He stepped over it and pulled Katie up behind him. Then they shone their torches round them. Where on earth were they?

CHAPTER 9

FOOTPRINTS – AND A LOCKED DOOR

The two children gazed around, amazed. They stood in a vast underground room, dark and low-roofed. Great wooden stands and shelves ran here and there, many of them broken and rotting.

"It's a cellar, Katie! That's what it is," said Nick at last. "Look, there are some old barrels over there. Maybe it was a wine cellar belonging to some big house."

"Nick, we can't be under the old ruined house on the cliff, can we?" said Katie, clutching his arm. "Those old places had huge cellars, you know. There's one at Holiday House – Mrs Potts told me, and she showed me the door down to it – a scary, big, dark place it looked."

"You may be right," said Nick, flashing his torch round. "We'll see if we can find steps leading upwards, Katie, and then we'll soon find out what house we're in."

He led the way into the gloomy, musty place. A large spider scuttled away, and some small animal, a mouse or a rat, pitter-pattered behind them. Katie kept close to Nick and held on to his arm.

Nick felt her shaking and he took her arm in his. "Don't worry, Katie," he said. "It's only a mouse."

The two children walked beside a line of wooden shelves, and came into a bare part of the cellars. Here old boxes and crates stood, covered with dust and cobwebs. Katie walked into a long cobweb and squealed when she felt it on her cheek, soft and clinging.

She brushed it away. "Oh, I'm silly," she said. "It was only a spider's web. Look, Nick, can those be steps leading upwards over there in that corner?"

They both shone their torches on the steps and then went towards them. They were ordinary stone cellar steps, and they led up to a stout wooden door.

Nick went first, hoping that the door would open easily. He gave it a push, but it didn't move.

"Oh no! It's locked," he said.

"There's a handle," said Katie, and pointed to it. Nick turned it this way and that – then suddenly there was a click and the door swung open!

"Come on," he said, and stumbled out into the daylight. He pulled Katie up, and they both gazed round. Where were they now?

They had no idea, except that they seemed to be standing in a stone-floored room with a huge, old-fashioned sink at one end. What looked like an ancient hand-pump stood near them. A low, dust-dimmed window let in the light.

"This is a scullery or kitchen, I think," said Nick. He went to the window and looked out. The sea lay there, heaving and glittering, immediately below him.

"We *are* in that old house," said Nick. "We must be. Come on, let's explore and then we'll know for sure."

"Nick – look!" said Katie suddenly, and she pointed at the floor. "Footprints! Someone else has been here."

There were many footprints, criss-crossing one another, showing up clearly in the thick dust. A trail of them led out of the door into a bigger room beyond, evidently another kitchen.

"A lot of people have been here," said Nick. "Or else one person has visited this place lots of times. I wonder why?"

"Let's follow the footprints," said Katie. So they trailed them out of the big kitchen and into a vast hall as big as the one at Holiday House.

"They go up the stairs," said Katie, suddenly beginning to whisper. "Look! Oh, Nick – you don't think whoever comes here is in the house now, do you?"

Nick stood and considered this. Then he listened hard, his head on one side like a dog's. Not a sound was to be heard except the wash of the sea outside.

"We'll chance it," said Nick in a whisper. "Be as quiet as you can."

They went up the stairs silently, following the footprints in the thick yellow dust. Up to a big landing, up more stairs, on to another landing, and up yet another, narrower stairway. A small landing was at the top, with four doors opening off. The footprints led to only one door. It was shut.

Nick walked cautiously to it, his feet

making no sound in the thick sandy dust. He tried the handle very, very carefully. It turned – but when he pushed against it the door did not open.

"Locked!" said Nick, with a groan. "Blow!"

"Is it locked from this side or the other side?" whispered Katie. "Look through the keyhole and see if there's a key in the other side."

Nick bent down and looked. There was no key the other side and he could easily see into part of the room. He stared in surprise, then stood back.

"You look, Katie," he said, "and tell me what you can see." Katie looked, in her turn, and then stood up, astonished.

"Nick! There's a mattress there – and a blanket. I could see part of them quite well. And I think I could make out a candlestick. Who sleeps here, in this old ruined house? And where are they? There's nobody there now. They've gone out, and locked the door behind them."

"They may be somewhere else in the house," said Nick, and for some reason this really scared the two children. Fear mingled with their excitement and they started off down the stairs, forgetting to be quiet and careful.

"I don't want to go down into the cellar again, and through that dark tunnel," panted Katie. "Isn't there any other way out, Nick?"

"There's a little door here with a key in it," said Nick, and ran to it. There were bolts at the top and bottom and he drew them back. They made a groaning sound, and Katie trembled. Nick turned the key and pulled hard at the door. With a sudden jerk it opened and he almost fell backwards. He took the key from the inner side of the door and pushed Katie out. He shut the door and locked it, putting the key into his pocket.

"We can't leave it open, or someone might get in," he said. "They could set fire to the place," he added, thinking of the mattress and blanket in the room at the top of the house.

They made their way into the sandy, desolate garden, and down the steep little path to the beach.

"The person who sleeps in that room must be the one we thought was Gareth," said Katie at last. "But it can't be Gareth, of course. He sleeps at Holiday House – and there wouldn't be any sense in his sleeping at that old house, would there?"

"None at all. I do wonder who it is," said Nick. "Katie, let's not tell anyone about this."

"No," agreed Katie, who had now recovered from her feeling of fear and was excited at having such a secret. "We won't tell a soul. But we'll get into that cave again and follow the passage in the opposite direction as soon as we can. And we'll keep watch on that room, Nick – at night, I mean. We'll be able to see if there's a light there if we look out of the window in that junk room at the bottom of the tower! I noticed that the window there looks right over to the old house!"

"Good idea," said Nick. "We'll keep watch tonight, Katie."

Punch went mad with joy to see them when they opened the door of their bedroom. He flew at them as if he hadn't seen them for weeks. "You'd have been scared stiff of those caves and that cellar, Punch," said Katie, hugging the little dog.

Nick suddenly remembered how Gareth had gone off by himself in the middle of the picnic and he wondered if he was feeling better. "I'll find out at teatime," he thought, as he washed himself thoroughly – the caves and cellars had dirtied him from head to foot.

Gareth came in to tea, looking more himself again. But he hardly said anything, and Mrs Holly glanced at him now and again, feeling worried. What a strange boy he was, with his moody silences! However, Clare made up for him, chattering on and on and on.

She had met a new family on the beach, and had made friends with them. "They've got an old aunt called Eliza," she said, "and this old aunt has a terrier just like yours, Nick."

"How do you know it's like ours?" said Nick, bored.

"And this family come from Halliwell," said Clare, "and their name is Lockham. I didn't like the big boy, he said a rude word, and—"

"That's enough, Clare," said her mother. "We really don't want to hear about boys who say rude things. Has everyone finished? Have you had plenty, Gareth dear? I never think you eat enough!"

It rained after tea, and Mrs Holly suggested that all the children should go into the big playroom and play games. Clare was pleased.

"I'll manage everything, Mum," she said. "I know how to get lots of games going – I do it at school for the little ones. You leave it to me."

And, before twenty minutes had passed, Clare had organised everyone into one big and successful party! She was a little nuisance, a big bore, and a dreadful nosy-parker – but she certainly knew how to boss all those small children and keep them as good as gold!

After supper, Katie and Nick went up to bed to read. They often did that, resting their legs, tired from swimming or running, reading an exciting book till it was time to go to sleep. Punch lay first on one bed and then on the other, giving each child licks in turn.

Tonight the two children did not intend to settle down to sleep as they usually did. No – as soon as it was dark they meant to creep out to the spiral staircase and go to the junk-room in the tower. They wanted to see if there was a light in that little top room in the old house!

"Are you ready, Katie?" called Nick at last. "Let's go then! And remember, don't make a sound!"

CHAPTER 10

A REAL PUZZLE

The two children left Punch in Nick's room and went quietly into the corridor. They walked to the end and went up the little spiral staircase to the first tower-room, where all the junk was kept.

They opened the door and went in. It was now dark, but Nick had his torch and switched it on. The room was not so full of junk and furniture as it had been when they last went into it – Mrs Holly had taken a good many of the chairs and tables out to use, now that it was half-term and Holiday House was almost full.

The children picked their way through the junk to the tower window. It was very dark indeed, as there was no moon. They looked out of the window, straight across to where the old house loomed like a black, solid shadow against the night sky.

It was completely dark from top to

bottom. Katie gave a little sigh of disappointment.

"Whoever it is is not there," she whispered. "What bad luck! Or do you suppose whoever was there has gone away now? Perhaps it was only a tramp, Nick – a tramp who comes now and again."

"Shh! Look!" said Nick excitedly. A light suddenly shone out from the top room they were watching. A flickering, uncertain light that was definitely candlelight.

"There you are," said Nick triumphantly. "There is someone there tonight. Hey – do you think that Gareth has ever noticed it? His window looks out across to the old house too! He might easily have seen it. Let's go and ask him."

They left the junk-room and went up the spiral staircase to Gareth's room, the middle one in the tower. They knocked at the closed door.

There was no answer at all. They knocked again. Still no answer. "He can't have gone to bed yet," said Katie. "He works till very late, Mrs Holly says."

"Look, there's a light in his room," said Nick, pointing to the crack of light under the door. "Let's go in. Perhaps he's just fallen asleep in his chair."

Nick opened the door and peeped in. Katie pushed in behind him. The children stared round, astonished. Nobody was there! The central light shone down on the table, but the room was quite empty, and the bed not yet slept in.

"He must have gone for a walk," said Nick. "Let's go and get undressed and then come back again."

But even when they came back again in half an hour's time there was no Gareth.

"It's weird," said Nick. "I know Mrs Holly locks the front door before this. How will he get in?"

"Let's sit in the junk-room and wait for him," said Katie. "We'll see him go past the door, and hear him too."

So they went to the junk-room and sat down on a sturdy crate. The light still shone in the top room of the old tower. Nick nudged Katie. "Do you suppose it's Gareth in that room?" he said. "You know we did think once that it was Gareth we saw there."

"No. It can't be," said Katie. "Why

should he go to that house to sleep when he's got his own room?"

"Listen!" said Nick, cocking his head. "Isn't that someone in Gareth's room now? I'm sure I heard a cough or something."

"But nobody's passed us and gone up the spiral stairs," said Katie. "If Gareth or anyone else had been up to the middle room we would have seen and heard them."

"All the same, there is someone there," said Nick. "And I'm going to see."

He went up the spiral stairway, followed by Katie – and as soon as they came to the shut door they heard a noise they knew very well indeed – Gareth's little cough!

"It *is* Gareth!" said Nick, in amazement. "But – but – how . . ."

Katie knocked on the door. Gareth called "Come in!" in rather a surprised voice, and looked even more surprised when he saw Nick and Katie wearing their dressing-gowns. "What's up?" he said.

"Gareth! You weren't here when we came a little while ago," said Nick, "and we sat in the junk-room and waited for you, but you didn't go up the stairs past the junk-room door – and yet here you are! How – how on earth did you manage to get here?"

Gareth stared at them and said nothing. He gave a quick glance out of the window, and Nick did too. He saw again the gleaming little light in the window of the top room of the distant house.

"Have you noticed that light before?" said Nick, his words tumbling out one on top of another. "We've been watching for it tonight – and we wanted to ask you if you'd spotted it, too. It's strange, isn't it?"

"Yes," said Gareth. His dark eyes looked at Nick and then away again. Nick went on eagerly.

"Gareth, we got into that old house today. We went upstairs – and we peeped through the keyhole of that room where there's a light, and . . ."

Gareth was listening intently, his eyes fixed on Nick. He sat quite still, his breath coming a little quickly.

"And what do you think we saw in the room?" said Nick.

"I – I can't imagine," said Gareth. "Tell me."

Nick told him about the mattress, the blanket and the candlestick. "What are they there for?" he asked Gareth. "Is it a tramp, do you think?"

"Possibly," said Gareth, looking out of the window. "Yes, possibly."

"We'd better tell Mrs Holly, hadn't we?" said Katie.

Gareth looked at her frowning. "No," he said. "Not just yet at any rate. We'll keep watch for a night or two more, shall we? I've never seen the light before tonight. Don't let's say anything yet. And now you'd better move off to bed. It's eleven o'clock and I've got some work to do. Goodnight."

"Well – goodnight then," said Nick, disappointed that Gareth had taken everything so calmly. Why, he hadn't even asked how he and Katie had got into the old house, and Nick was simply longing to explain about the cave and the tunnel.

He and Katie went out of the door and shut it quietly. They went back to their own rooms and Nick joined Katie, curling up on her bed.

"Gareth's never excited about anything," he said. "He's very dull to tell things to, isn't he, Katie? I was so excited at seeing that light."

"Nick, don't you think it's peculiar that Gareth didn't tell us how he got into his room without us seeing him?" said Katie slowly. "He never said a word about that – not a single word."

"You're right!" said Nick. "I was so excited about that light in the window that I forgot about trying to make him tell us how he got back. After all, there's no way to his room except up the spiral stairs!"

"Or down them," said Katie. "But the top tower-room is locked, so he couldn't have come from there. How did he get back – or was he hiding under the bed or in his wardrobe when we went in the first time?"

"Now you're muddling me," said Nick. "I must be getting sleepy. Oh, let's leave this mystery for tonight and sleep on it. We may have some good ideas about it tomorrow. I'm going to bed. Goodnight, Katie!"

Off he went and Katie heard his bed creaking as he settled down in it. She lay and thought about the exciting happenings of the day. The cave, the tunnel, the cellars, the old empty house, the top room, locked, and furnished with just a few things. And then the mystery of Gareth going out for a walk and getting back to his room unseen by them. What did it all mean?

Well, perhaps it wasn't a mystery after all – perhaps there was some simple explanation. But Gareth was odd – Clare was quite right. Gloomy Gareth really was very odd.

Gareth seemed quite all right the next day at breakfast and didn't say a word about the happenings of the night before. The children were not surprised at this, because Clare was nearby all the time.

"We'll watch for the light again tonight," said Nick to Katie. "Let's go and tell Gareth, and ask if he'll watch with us."

But Gareth was not in his room, and Mrs Holly told them he had gone off for the day to do some shopping.

"New socks and swimming trunks or something," she said. "I was glad he wanted to go – a whole day off will be a change for him. He'll have a breakdown if he doesn't take time off now and again!"

Gareth appeared at suppertime, looking white and tired. He said very little about his day and didn't seem to have enjoyed it much.

"Oh, I just did a bit of shopping, and mooched around the town and went to a cinema," he said. "I feel a bit tired, so I'll turn in early, I think, Mrs Holly."

The two children followed him when they left the supper table, with Punch trotting behind them.

"Gareth!" said Nick in a loud whisper, as they came into the corridor where their rooms were. "Gareth! Shall we watch for the light to shine in the old house tonight?"

"You watch if you like," said Gareth. "I really feel too tired." He went up to his room and shut the door. Punch gave a growl as if to say, "What a grouch!" and the children felt like growling too!

Gruff the cat slid out of the shadows near Punch and gave him a sudden slap with his paw. Punch yelped and looked round, but Gruff had gone.

"Chase him, then!" said Katie, knowing quite well that Punch wouldn't. "Cowardy-custard! Come on downstairs, Nick – it's not dark enough yet to watch for that light."

Later on, in slippers and dressing-gowns, they crept up the spiral stairs to the junk-room and settled themselves down by the window.

"There's no light yet," said Nick in disappointment. "Let's wait a while and see if it appears."

But it didn't. The old house remained dark from attic to cellar, and the children went to bed disappointed.

"There's no mystery any more," said Nick. "It must be a tramp who sometimes uses that room, that's all. Bother, I did enjoy that bit of excitement, didn't you, Katie? I wish it hadn't all fizzled out."

"Oh well – perhaps something else will come along," said Katie. "We'll keep our eyes and ears open."

She didn't know how right she was! Things began to happen the very next day!

CHAPTER 11

TROUBLE

The trouble began at about teatime. Mrs Holly heard loud voices coming from the kitchen, and went out to see what was the matter.

Mrs Potts and Mrs Tomms were arguing angrily. "I tell you, I made five meat pies and now one has gone!" said Mrs Potts.

"Well, what about my cakes, then?" said Mrs Tomms, in her loud bark of a voice. "Where's that fruitcake I made? Not a slice cut out of it even – and it's vanished."

"Now, now – whatever is all this?" said Mrs Holly. "Something missing?"

"Yes, Mrs Holly!" said both women at once, and told her at the tops of their voices, so that she had to put her hands to her ears.

"Well, I'm sorry about it," said Mrs Holly at last. "It's a puzzle where a cake and a meat pie could have gone. I don't suspect anyone of stealing them, though. Do you?"

"Well, yes, I do," said Mrs Tomms grimly. "There's too many children come into this kitchen, Mrs Holly. That's what I say!"

Clare came in at the door, curious to know what the argument was about. Mrs Tomms scowled at her.

"And here's one of them!" she said, nodding at Clare. "Always prying and peeping about, that one. In my fridge, too, last night – oh yes, I saw her!"

"I was only looking to see if all the trifle was finished up last night!" said Clare, scowling back. "Sometimes Mum lets me finish things up."

"You didn't finish up a meat pie and a fruitcake, I suppose?" said Mrs Tomms, who had taken a real dislike to the bossy little girl.

"Now, Mrs Tomms, that's enough," said Mrs Holly, in her cool, firm voice. "I can't have you accusing my daughter of a thing like that. We must just keep a good watch, that's all, and find out who it is. No child may come into the kitchen from now on, not even you, Clare! We do sometimes have trouble with hungry children, Mrs Potts, don't we? They come in after swimming, absolutely ravenous, and raid the fridge!"

"Yes, that's right. It often happens," said Mrs Potts. "But a whole meat pie – good gracious!"

Mrs Holly left the kitchen and took Clare with her. Clare looked rather white. "I want you to come into my room, Clare," said Mrs Holly.

They went in and Mrs Holly shut the door. Before she could say anything, Clare burst into a torrent of words, tears pouring down her face.

"I know what you're going to say! You're going to say it's me! Just because I've sometimes taken a biscuit or two, or some jelly to finish up! You think it's me, don't you? You don't like me, Mum, you like the other children, you're always nice to them, especially the – the—"

"Clare!" said her mother in horror. "Whatever are you saying? Of course I like you. And I wouldn't dream of thinking it was you who stole a meat pie. You know I love you and trust you! What's the matter with you?"

She put her arms round Clare and gave her a hug. "Aren't you silly! You know I have to be nice to all the other children, unless they're impossible, like John was! After all, Clare, this is our livelihood – running Holiday House for children – isn't it?"

Clare suddenly felt better. She'd always worried about her mother preferring the other children who came to stay in the house. She dabbed her eyes and looked at the ground. "But – but – often you let the others do things you won't let me do – you never scold them if they tell lies, you—"

"No – because I'm not their mother, nor their teacher," said Mrs Holly. "Sometimes they come with their own mothers and sometimes with nannies or aunties or grannies. I can't interfere in the way they are being brought up, Clare – it's their mothers and nannies and grannies who must tell them off, not me. You must see that!"

"But do you want to tell them off?" asked Clare. "Sometimes I think it's only me you want to get cross with – and you never make a fuss of me like you make a fuss of the others, Mum, do you?"

"No. I'd like to – but you're such a prickly little person!" said her mother. "And believe me, I certainly would love to tell off that naughty child Peter, and that selfish Jane, and send George out of the room when he behaves so badly at meals. But I'm not their mother, so I can't."

Clare dried her eyes. "I think I am a bit prickly," she said. "I often think I'm not a nice person at all really – like Katie and Nick are, I mean. You like them, don't you?"

"Yes. So do you," said Mrs Holly. "But I wouldn't change this prickly little girl for any other child in the world; so now you know!"

"Oh, Mum!" said Clare, and her face shone. "I never thought that."

"No. You've been jealous, haven't you?" said her mother. "And if you're jealous you can't possibly see what is true and what is not. Now, listen. I brought you in here because I want you to help me with something. Mrs Allen, George's mother, has told me that she's lost her pretty brooch, the one with the little blue sapphire in the centre. She's worried about it – and I want you to hunt everywhere for it. Will you?"

"Oh, yes. Of course," said Clare. "So that's why you brought me in here. I thought you were going to get cross with me! I'll go and look for the brooch now. I know where Mrs Allen sat on the beach yesterday – it may be in the sand there."

Clare ran off. Mrs Holly smiled and sighed at the same time. What a pity Clare had to share her with so many other children! Well, perhaps this talk had made her happier. She thought about the things taken from the kitchen fridge. Who could have gone off with a meat pie and a fruitcake? She hoped that Mrs Allen's brooch had been lost, not stolen. It was very difficult to work happily when there was a possible thief in the house, and everyone suspected everyone else.

Holiday House was very full now and Mrs Holly planned something exciting for the older ones each day. There were long walks to interesting places, picnics, coach rides to different beaches, parties and dances. It was really very exciting, and

Katie and Nick loved every minute.

They were so tired at night that they couldn't even keep watch on the old house to see if the light was still shining there! Three nights went by, and they almost forgot about it, though they often talked about the cave and its exciting hole leading to the tunnel in the cliff.

And then one morning Clare came into their room, looking very mysterious, with her finger to her lips. The children looked at her in surprise.

"What is it? Why are you looking like that?" asked Nick, shutting his book.

"My mum said I could come and ask you to help us," said Clare, looking important and speaking in a very low voice.

"Well, what is it?" said Nick again. "And why are you speaking like that? Nobody can possibly hear you in our rooms!"

"Even walls have ears," said Clare. "Haven't you heard that saying?"

"In that case we'd better go down to the beach," said Katie. "There are no walls there!"

"Please listen," said Clare. "Mum's very, very worried, because if something isn't done about it she's got to get the police in to Holiday House!"

That made Nick and Katie sit up at once! "Worried about what?" said Nick impatiently. "And why the police?"

"Well – things keep disappearing," said Clare. "Food out of the kitchen, for instance – some goes almost every day, you know. And Mrs Allen's brooch went; and Nanny Hurst's bracelet; and now Mum's watch has gone. Her nice gold one."

"Oh no! That's awful," said Nick. "Do you mean they've been stolen? Who can the thief be?"

"That's what we want to find out," said Clare. "Mum says that it's much easier for us children to keep a watch because we're always running in and out of the rooms and we go everywhere. We must keep our eyes open and report anything unusual to her. Anyone going into someone else's room, and so on, and—"

"Are any other children going to watch?" asked Katie. "Because if we all know, it would be silly."

"Oh no – only you two," said Clare. "You two and me."

"What about Gareth?" said Katie. "He's been here a long time and he knows the whole house. Can't we tell him, too?"

"No. Certainly not," said Clare.

She had put on a most peculiar look and the children stared at her in surprise.

"What do you mean?" said Nick at last. "Don't be so mysterious, Clare. I don't see why we can't tell Gareth. He's been looking so worried lately that it would do him good to have something exciting to think about."

"No. *Not* Gareth!" said Clare.

"Anyone would think you thought he was the thief," said Katie, annoyed.

"Well – perhaps I do think that!" said Clare, and turned to go out of the room. But Nick ran to her and caught her arm.

"You can't say a thing like that, and then just walk out of the room!" he said. "That's a horrible thing to say – that poor Gareth is a thief! You just take it back."

"No, I shan't," said Clare. "I've seen him creeping about at night – and I'm sure he sneaks down to the kitchen. I saw someone coming out of there last night, and it looked just like Gareth."

"How do you know? Were all the lights

on?" asked Nick, in a disbelieving voice.

"No. It was dark," said Clare. "Anyway, somebody else thinks it's Gareth – she's seen him creeping about too!"

"Who?" asked Nick. "I thought you said that no other children knew about this."

"They don't. It's Lydia who told me!" said Clare triumphantly. "She's very, very worried about it because she may be suspected of stealing things – she has to go into most of the rooms to make beds and dust! She thinks it's Gareth!"

"Well, I don't," said Nick. "And instead of snooping and prying on him, I'm going to tell him everything and ask him to help. See?"

"You mustn't," said Clare, lowering her voice so that it could hardly be heard. "Lydia told me something else. Something dreadful! Shall I tell you what it is?"

CHAPTER 12

THE MAN WITH YELLOW HAIR

The two children stared at Clare, wondering what to say. They really didn't want to hear any more nasty things about Gareth, strange and gloomy though he always was. Clare grew impatient.

"So – shall I tell you this dreadful thing that Lydia knows about Gareth, or not?"

"You'd better tell us," said Nick. "But if it isn't true I'll go straight to your mother about it, Clare. So be careful."

"Oh – it is true," said Clare. "It was in the papers, Lydia said. Well, Gareth's brother is a thief – a burglar! And he's been sent away, to some very strict place – not prison, he's not old enough – and he's got to be there for a long time."

The children didn't know what to say. It certainly was a sad piece of news. Poor Gareth! He had got a brother after all, but he was ashamed of him, and so he didn't talk about him at all – he'd even said that he hadn't got a brother when Clare had gone to ask him. No wonder he'd been angry with her for prying into his secret!

"Well," said Clare, "aren't you going to say anything? Don't you believe me?"

"Yes, I think I do believe you," said Nick. "It all seems to fit in with Gareth's behaviour – he's so depressed and keeps himself to himself, and hardly ever talks. But just because he's got a bad brother, it doesn't mean that he's a thief, too, Clare."

"Lydia says he's as bad as his brother," said Clare obstinately. "And do you know how she knows? Because her brother knew Gareth and his brother well. He was a trainee gardener at their school. Lydia's brother's called Sam and she thinks he's great. Well, after all I've told you, will you help to keep a watch on Gareth? It's a shame that Lydia might be suspected of being the thief, if all the time it's Gareth."

"No, I will not! I'm certainly not going to spy on Gareth," said Nick. "Nor is Katie. This is only Lydia's story! Gareth may not even have a brother – it's only Lydia who says so."

"The woman at the sweet shop told me, too. Don't you remember?" said Clare. "Oh, it's true all right. Okay, if you won't be sensible and spy on Gareth, I will. But you could keep a look out and see if you notice anything unusual at any time."

"We'll do that," said Nick, and opened his book and began to read again. Clare took the hint and went out of the room, giving the door a good slam. She was cross.

"Bother Clare and her gossip," said Nick, putting his book down. "What do you think, Katie?"

"I'm really sorry for poor Gareth," said Katie. "And I don't think for one moment he would steal anything. But as things seem to be disappearing, we might as well keep our eyes open and try and catch the real thief!"

"Right. I agree. I hate the way Clare gloats when she has anything unkind to tell."

"Let's go out and find Punch," said Katie. "He's probably with the little kids. He enjoys that so much we hardly ever see him now!"

They went out in their swimsuits to find

Punch. He was on the beach with a group of two- and three-year-olds, and he was having a wonderful time. The small ones loved the playful little dog, and ran after him all the time.

He bounded up to Katie and Nick. "Come for a walk, Punch," said Katie, and the little terrier, barking excitedly, jumped up at her. They set off along the beach.

"Let's swim," said Katie. "There's a deep pool here by the rock – it's wonderful and it'll be as hot as a bath!"

They lay down in the warm pool, resting their heads against the rock behind. "Ugh! A shrimp's tickling me – or is it a crab?" said Katie. "This is fabulous. I could stay here for hours!"

They lay there, enjoying the warm water, till a little cold wave ran into their pool and made a ripple. "Tide's coming in," said Nick, sitting up. "Look, Katie, we've got a good view of the ruined house up on the cliff. I wonder if the old tramp, or whoever it is, is still using that top room for a camping-out place."

"Yes. I wonder, too," said Katie. "Let's go up into the garden and see if we can find any footprints. We couldn't before, but we might now."

They got out of the pool and, warmed by the sun, they climbed up the cliff path. They were soon in the sandy garden, and searched the ground eagerly.

"Hey, look – some fresh footprints!" said Katie, pointing to a trail of big ones that wandered here and there.

"Yes, those look new," said Nick. "Someone with pretty heavy boots has made them. A hiker, maybe."

They sat themselves down in a warm corner to dry their swimming things. The sun was so hot that it didn't take long. They were just about to get up and go when Katie heard a sound.

She put her hand on Nick's arm. "Someone's coming," she whispered. "Let's see who it is. It may be the person who uses the top room where the light shone."

So they kept very quiet. Soon a young man came round the corner of the house, a slouching youth with chewing-gum in his mouth. He had fair hair that was brushed back from his face and tied in a ponytail.

He stood looking up at the house and

then went to the garden door where the
children had made their escape from the
old house a few days before. He tried the
handle and then shook the door. He walked
back into the garden again – and suddenly

saw the two children sitting in the sun.

"Hi!" he said, looking startled. "I never saw you. What are you doing here?"

"Just drying ourselves after swimming," said Nick. "What are you doing here?"

"Oh, just looking round this old house," said the young man. His curiously soft voice didn't seem to go with his sharp eyes. "Do you know who owns it?"

"No," said Nick.

"I suppose you haven't seen anyone about, have you?" said the young man.

"How do you mean?" asked Nick cautiously, thinking of the camper up in the top room.

"Er – in the garden here, for instance," said the young man.

"No," said Nick again. "Why? Are you looking for someone?"

The young man didn't answer. He was getting some more chewing-gum out of a packet. He threw away the paper, put the gum in his mouth and waved to the children. Then he turned round and disappeared down the cliff path.

"Who was he, do you suppose?" said Katie, in a low voice. "Was he looking for the person up in the top room?"

"I shouldn't think so," said Nick. "I don't know."

"I didn't like him," said Katie. "Long greasy hair and dirty fingernails."

"I didn't like his eyes. Did you notice that he never looked at us properly, Katie?" said Nick. "He kept glancing around all the time."

"Well, we needn't tell Clare about him!" said Katie. "Or shall we?"

"No, he can't have anything to do with Holiday House," said Nick. "Come on. We must go. Mrs Holly's very sweet and kind, but she does get cross if we're late for meals."

After lunch Mrs Holly called to them. "Nick! Katie! Will you two go and pick some strawberries and gooseberries for some pies? You will? Thank you!"

The children loved picking fruit, especially as they were allowed to eat some as they picked. They took two baskets from the rack and lined them with cabbage leaves so that the fruit wouldn't stain the baskets. Mrs Holly was very particular about things like that!

They were just going off to the kitchen garden to begin their job when Clare came up to them, looking mysterious. "I've got some peculiar news," she said.

"What?" asked the children.

"Well, what do you think Mrs Potts found on the top shelf of the larder today?" said Clare.

"A dead beetle," said Nick, grinning.

"A mouse," said Katie.

"No. She found a little pile of money," said Clare. "And she says it wasn't there when she cleaned the shelf yesterday. She says she didn't put it there, and nor did Mrs Tomms."

"Perhaps it's the thief, paying for his food!" said Nick, with a laugh.

"Don't be silly," said Clare. "But it's peculiar, isn't it? Don't you think so?"

"Not very," said Nick. "Probably one of the kitchen staff put the money there for a moment and then forgot all about it. Are you going to pick fruit with us, Clare?"

"Yes. I'll get a basket and join you in half a minute," said Clare, and ran off, disappointed that the children didn't think much of her news.

Katie and Nick went into the quiet kitchen garden, where strawberry plants red with berries grew alongside the prickly gooseberry bushes. Next to these were the tall raspberry canes, thick and bushy, with the first raspberries already ripening on them.

Nick slipped in between two high rows of raspberry canes to pick a few berries, and then stopped in surprise. Someone was hiding there. Someone who slipped quickly out of the other end of the row and ran off through a door in the kitchen garden wall.

"Katie! Did you see who that was?" said Nick, pushing his way through to where she was picking gooseberries. She was looking very startled.

"Yes, I did – oh, Nick, it was that young man we saw by the old ruined house just before we came home for lunch," she said. "What's he doing here?"

"I thought I recognised his long fair hair," said Nick. "Well, this is really peculiar. You're right, Katie, what *is* he doing here?"

CHAPTER 13

GARETH TELLS A SECRET

The children had no time to discuss the yellow-haired young man who had so strangely hidden in the raspberry canes, because at that moment Clare came up with her basket. Nick looked at Katie and shook his head slightly. She knew what he meant.

"He doesn't want me to tell Clare about the young man yet," she thought, and she didn't say a word.

Clare, of course, talked non-stop as she always did. "Mrs Tomms says this – Lydia says that – and I think so and so – and don't you suppose . . ." On and on she went without giving the other two a chance to say a word. Not that they minded. But they pricked up their ears when she repeated one thing that Lydia had said.

"Lydia says that Gareth's room ought to be searched. She says that she's sure he's got stolen things hidden there . . ."

"Well, she'd better not start searching the room herself, because if Gareth discovers her there – or you either – he'll fly into the biggest rage you've ever seen him in!" said Nick at once. "Lydia has no right to talk like that, Clare. Nobody has any right to accuse another person without real proof. You're as bad as Lydia!"

Clare sulked. Then she began again. "Well, something else disappeared last night – Mrs Thomas has just reported it to Mum. Her daughter's locket has gone. Mrs Thomas says she knows she put it into the top drawer, and now it's gone. There's somebody getting through windows or doors, no doubt about it."

The children had the same thought at once. Could it be that fair-haired man? After all, he had no business to be hiding in the garden, he must have been up to no good. If only they could catch him stealing something, they could prove that Clare was wrong – that it wasn't Gareth!

Where had he gone? Was he even now skulking about to find something to steal? Nick looked at his full basket and made up his mind. He would take his basket to the kitchen and give in the fruit he had picked – but instead of coming back to pick some more, he would do a little skulking round himself!

"I'm going to take in my fruit!" he called to the girls, and ran off. Mrs Tomms was pleased to see so many strawberries and gave him one of her newly-made buns. Off he went again, his rubber-soled trainers making no noise at all.

There were no children in the back garden of the house – they were all either on the beach or in the front garden in their pushchairs, where there was plenty of shade in the hot afternoons. Nick had the place to himself. He wriggled into the middle of a lilac bush and stayed there, quite silent, making a little spyhole for himself.

He could see almost all round him. From the distant kitchen garden he could hear Clare's sudden laugh, but otherwise all was peaceful and quiet. No birds sang, not even the little chaffinch who sometimes trilled his *chip-chip-cherry-erry-chippy-ooo-ee-ar* song from the top of a bush.

Nick kept absolutely still – and then he heard a noise. What was it? He peeped through his hole – and saw the fair-haired man coming silently along the path, looking back every now and again to make sure he wasn't followed. He passed Nick's bush without a glance, and went on quietly towards the end of the house, where the big tower rose up. Nick made another spyhole and watched him. He saw with astonishment that the man was now climbing up the strong ivy stems that covered the tower. Where was he going?

The man climbed to the first window – the window of the junk-room – and peered inside. Then he began climbing up to the second window.

At that moment who should come padding along the path but Punch. He stopped by the lilac bush where Nick was hiding and sniffed hard, looking puzzled. Then he leaped into the bush and barked madly, thinking that Nick was having one of his games of hide-and-seek with him.

The fair-haired man slid rapidly down the ivy as soon as he heard Punch barking, and dropped to the ground. He ran for the wall and climbed over it, just as Punch realised that there was someone to chase.

The little terrier raced over to the wall and barked again, trying his hardest to jump up the bricks.

Gareth put his head out of the tower window. "Stop Punch barking!" he called irritably. "How can I work with that row going on?"

Nick ran to the tower. "Gareth! Someone was climbing up the ivy to your window just now and Punch barked at him."

"What? Climbing up the ivy?" said Gareth, astonished. "Come up and tell me about it."

Soon Nick and Punch were in the middle tower-room with Gareth. It was as untidy as ever, with books and papers all over the place.

"I was hiding in the lilac bush," began Nick, quite out of breath with his quick climb up the spiral staircase to Gareth's room. "And this man came by – and he suddenly began to climb up the ivy—"

"What was he like?" asked Gareth quickly.

"He slouched," said Nick. "And he had long fair hair tied back in a ponytail, with a soft sort of voice."

"Oh no!" said Gareth with a moan and, to Nick's surprise, he put his face down into his hands. "I was afraid it was."

"What's the matter, Gareth?" asked Nick. "Do you know who he is, then?"

"Yes," said Gareth, still with his head in his hands. "It's Sam."

"Sam?" said Nick. "Who's he? Oh – is he Lydia's brother? Of course. They're really alike, fair hair and soft voices! Why didn't I think of it before?"

"He's the meanest, cleverest, most dishonest person in the world!" said Gareth. There was a pause and then he went on.

"Nick, what have you been hearing about me? I know things have been said. Tell me truthfully, and then I'll try and explain a few things to you."

Nick sat down in a chair, and Punch leaped on to his knees. "Right, Gareth," he said. "I've been wanting to talk to you about a few things, actually. First, Clare says that Lydia told her you've got a brother who's a thief and has been put away somewhere but not in prison because he's not old enough."

"Anything else?" said Gareth, his face very white.

"Yes, Lydia has told Clare, and I suppose she's told others as well, that you're a thief too, and it's you who's stealing the things that keep being nicked from Holiday House."

"I see," said Gareth. "Do you think I'm the thief, Nick?"

"No."

There was a silence and then Gareth began to speak again in a low voice. "I *have* got a brother – although I told Clare I hadn't. And he's been sent to a young offenders' institution far away from here, because they said he had broken into a safe and stolen a case of valuable jewellery. But he didn't steal it. Sam stole it."

"How do you know?" said Nick. "Why didn't Sam own up, then?"

"Peter, my brother, and I were at boarding-school," began Gareth. "He was a dare-devil – you know, the sort of person who does things nobody else ever thinks of or dares to do. He's great, Nick – he's the sort of bloke who'll get the VC or some other medal for courage and daring when he's grown up. He's older than I am, and I thought the world of him. I still do."

"Your parents are dead, aren't they?" said Nick. "So I suppose your brother meant a lot to you."

"Yes, he did, I looked up to him no end; he was really all I had," said Gareth. "Well, he got friendly with Sam, who was a trainee gardener at the school – and Sam was a bit of a dare-devil too. He and Peter once climbed up to the top of the school tower and hung the headmaster's hat on the flag-pole – that's the sort of thing Peter did!"

He paused. "Well," he continued, "to cut a long story short, Sam promised he would show Peter how to open a safe; he was clever at that sort of thing. He said it would be fun to stuff the safe full of cabbages and potatoes and carrots and see what would happen when the head opened the safe and found them inside!"

Nick gave a small laugh. "That's quite funny really," he said.

"Yes – but it didn't turn out to be at all funny," said Gareth. "Because when the head opened the safe the next day, certainly the vegetables were all there in full array –

but the case with his wife's diamond necklace, brooches and earrings was gone!"

Nick gasped. "What happened then?" he asked.

"The works!" said Gareth. "Pete owned up that he had opened the safe with Sam just to play a joke – but said, of course, that he knew nothing of the jewellery case. But the beast of a Sam swore that he had been with Lydia, his sister, at the time the safe was opened – around midnight – and said that he knew nothing about it."

"How absolutely dreadful!" said Nick, horrified.

"So Pete was taken off by the police and he was sent to this place where boys too young for prison go. It's not as bad as prison but he's shut away and is learning to be a carpenter instead of working to go to university. I had to leave the school too and come here instead to cram with a tutor for my exams. Sam lost his job, as the headmaster said he obviously couldn't be trusted, and that made Sam very bitter towards Peter. He went up to Scotland or somewhere to work for his uncle till everything had blown over, but now he's

137

back again, as you see. I didn't know he lived near Holiday House or I wouldn't have come here."

"Was the jewellery ever found?" asked Nick.

"No! It's obvious that Sam's got it safely hidden away somewhere till he thinks it's safe to try and sell it," said Gareth.

"What's he snooping round here for?" asked Nick, after a pause. "Just to worry you and upset us?"

"No. He didn't know I was here at Holiday House till Lydia happened to take a job as cleaner – and she told him, of course," said Gareth. "And do you know why he's spying round everywhere? I oughtn't to tell you, but I shall go crazy if I don't tell someone!"

"Tell me," said Nick. "I won't split on you, Gareth."

"Well," said Gareth, dropping his voice, and looking desperately at Nick, "well, my brother ran away from the institution where he'd been sent and came to me. And I'm hiding him, Nick. I couldn't do anything else, could I?"

"No, you couldn't," said Nick, extremely

startled. "Especially as he's innocent. How does Sam know he's escaped, though?"

"It was in the papers," said Gareth. "As soon as I knew he'd escaped, I guessed he would come to me, and I went over to Tiddington, where Sam lives – that was the day you all thought I'd gone shopping – and I begged Sam to own up to the robbery, and to tell me where he's hidden the jewellery. I couldn't bear to think of Pete being caught and sent back to that place again. But Sam only laughed at me."

"The beast," said Nick. "And now I suppose he's hoping to find that you've hidden Peter somewhere, so that he can go to the police and tell them to get in their good books. Katie and I saw him snooping round the old house this morning, and . . . and . . . Oh, Gareth, you've hidden your brother in the room at the top of the old ruined house, haven't you?"

Gareth nodded. "Yes, that's where he is. That's why I was so upset when you saw the light of his candle the other night, Nick. But what am I to do now?"

CHAPTER 14

NICK AND KATIE ARE VERY CLEVER

Nick stared at Gareth, feeling very sorry for him. He thought of Peter, shut up in the little top room that Gareth had so carefully prepared for him when he'd heard that he'd escaped, guessing that he would be coming for help.

"Gareth, who's stealing things at Holiday House now – do you know?" he asked. "Is that Sam too?"

"No. I'm sure it's Lydia," said Gareth. "She's as bad as Sam. She was a cleaner near him at another school, and things disappeared there too. If it hadn't been for her telling the police that Sam was with her at the time of the burglary, my brother would never have been found guilty."

"Where do you suppose the jewellery is now?" said Nick, after a pause.

"Well hidden somewhere near Sam's home at Tiddington," said Gareth. "I expect he'll be digging it up, wherever it is, and trying to sell it, now he's back from Scotland."

A loud noise sounded through the window and both boys jumped violently. Punch leaped off Nick's knee and barked.

"The gong for tea!" said Nick. "It really made me jump. I've been here ages, Gareth."

"Don't tell anyone what I've told you," begged Gareth.

"Only my sister Katie," promised Nick. "We tell each other everything. And if you want any help from us at any time, let me know. We're absolutely on your side!"

"Thanks," said Gareth, looking slightly more cheerful. "Don't let that snoopy little Clare guess anything, though. And watch out for Sam. Let me know whenever you see him. Spy on him if you can, in case he finds out Pete's hiding place. I couldn't bear that!"

"Come on down to tea," said Nick, standing up. Gareth shook his head.

"No. I don't want any. Give Mrs Holly my apologies, and say I'm quite all right."

Nick ran down the spiral stairs, his head

in a whirl. What a story! He must tell Katie as soon as possible. But how? Clare might come along at any moment – there was no getting away from her, especially after tea!

Katie was glad to see him. "Wherever have you been all afternoon?" she said, and stopped suddenly when he gave her a little kick under the table.

After tea they went up to their rooms, and Nick shut the door carefully. "Let's go into your room," he said to Katie, "and we'll shut your door too – then if Clare comes snooping along she won't hear us talking."

They sat on Katie's bed and Nick told his sister all that he'd heard from Gareth. She listened wide-eyed.

"Oh, what a dreadful story!" she said. "Poor Gareth! That horrible Sam! Why didn't we realise he was Lydia's brother this morning, they're exactly alike! I bet Lydia is the one who's been stealing the things here. I wonder where she's hiding everything – not in her room – she would be afraid of it being searched!"

Punch jumped down from the bed and whined. "Shh!" said Nick, sure that the terrier had heard Clare at the outer door. "Don't make a sound, Punch!"

Punch stood and listened, then jumped back on the bed again.

"Clare's gone!" said Katie, with a grin.

"Thanks for the warning, Punch. Nick, what do you suppose will happen about Gareth's brother? He can't stay hidden for weeks. What a horrible life for him!"

"No wonder Gareth's been so gloomy and mysterious and quiet," said Nick. "Well, that's everything, I think, Katie. Let's go down – and be sure to keep a look-out for that horrid Sam, with his long yellow ponytail."

They went out into the garden, and decided to play at the bottom where there was a small hayfield. Punch raced in front and then stopped dead at the hedge and gave a growl.

"What's the matter?" said Nick. "What's up, Punch? Found a hedgehog or something – or is it old Gruff lying in wait for birds?"

Punch barked, and someone stood up behind the hedge. The children caught sight of a head of yellow hair – Sam! He recognised them as the two children he had seen in the garden of the old house that morning.

"Hey, you," he said. "Can you give a message to my sister Lydia for me? I haven't been able to get hold of her today. Tell her I want to see her this evening, about half past ten, on the beach under the caves, okay?"

"I'll tell her," said Nick, and Sam slunk away. Nick turned to face Katie, his eyes gleaming and his face scarlet.

"We'll tell Lydia to meet him – and we'll be there, too, Katie!" he said. "We'll listen to what Sam has to say – he might even tell her where he's hidden the jewellery!"

"But where can we hide?" asked Katie.

"There are plenty of rocks there," said Nick, "and it'll be dark. We can hide behind the rock nearest to Sam and Lydia when we see them meet."

Katie felt excited. This meant that they would have to creep out quite late, as darkness was falling! She looked so excited that Clare kept asking her all the evening what was the matter!

It seemed a very long time to wait, once

they were in bed. "We'd better creep out about a quarter past ten – in case Sam or Lydia are early," said Nick. "We'll take Punch. He's always perfectly quiet if we want him to be."

At a quarter past ten the children went silently out of their room and into the corridor. They unlocked the little garden door downstairs, shut it, and went out into the warm darkness. Nick had a torch to light their way. They went down to the beach, with Punch walking quietly at their heels, delighted at this unexpected outing.

"Here are the caves," whispered Nick. "And there's a really big rock. Let's stand behind it till we hear the others coming."

They stood there, listening, but hearing nothing except the soft murmuring of the waves further down on the sand. And then Punch gave a small growl, and the children knew that someone was coming.

It had to be Sam, because they could see his pale hair shining faintly in the darkness. He walked right by them and went to a sandy place below the caves. He sat down.

Almost immediately Lydia came, looking

like a ghost in her white coat. She gave a low whistle and Sam answered. She saw him sitting down and went over to him.

"We'll slip across to the next rock," whispered Nick. "We'll hear better then."

They made no noise in the soft sand as they crept over to the rock near Sam and Lydia. Punch made no sound either. They heard Sam's voice as soon as they came near.

"Yeah, I know where Peter is now – Gareth's hiding him in one of the top rooms of that old house. I'm going up there tonight to frighten the life out of him! I'm going to tell him I'm fetching the police there tomorrow. That'll make him squirm!"

"How did you find out?" said Lydia.

"I saw the light there when I came down here tonight," said Sam. "I thought that old house might make a good hiding place – and when I saw the light I knew I was right."

"Sam, what about the jewellery?" asked Lydia, dropping her voice a little. "You said the place you'd hidden it over in Tiddington wasn't safe any longer."

"That's right," said Sam. "I'd buried the

case in a field that's going to be built over now, and I was afraid someone would find it. So I've brought it over here, Lydia. Can you keep it safe somewhere so that I can get my hands on it when I want it?"

"Oh no, Sam! I'd be scared to have it anywhere at Holiday House, especially now there's people snooping round looking for the missing things," said Lydia. "I did hear that the police were coming tomorrow to question us all. But I've got my little lot safe and nobody can find them."

"Where did you put the things you took?" asked Sam.

Lydia gave a giggle. "Not far from here, Sam. There's a cave just behind us, with a rocky shelf right at the top. That's where I've put everything I pinched."

"Good idea," said Sam. "Look, take the jewellery case, Lydia. You put all your things into it, and then hide the case on the rocky shelf you've just told me about. I'll fetch it when I'm ready."

"Let's put it there now," said Lydia. "I don't want to take anything back to Holiday House." They stood up and Sam suddenly switched on a torch. Luckily the light didn't go anywhere near the children's hiding place.

Sam went to the cave with his sister. It was not one that the children had explored. They watched eagerly from behind their rock, and Nick determined to get that jewellery case as soon as he could. What a piece of luck! It would have in it not only the jewellery taken from the school safe but all the things that Lydia had stolen from Holiday House!

Sam and his sister were not in the cave very long. They soon came out and sat talking. "Right, I'm going along to that old house now, to frighten Peter rigid," said Sam at last. "What do you suppose he'll say when I knock on his door and say 'Peter! Guess who this is! It's Sam!'"

Lydia giggled. "He'll be terrified – he'll think he's having a nightmare, Sam!" She thought it was very funny. She got to her feet, giggling, and straightened her coat. "Well, I must be off. Goodbye.'"

She glided away, a white blur in the darkness. Sam went off towards the old house, whistling softly. Nick gave Katie a nudge.

"Katie! Did you hear all that? How incredibly lucky we came down here!"

"Let's look for the jewellery case!" Katie whispered back excitedly. "Quick, let's search that cave."

They made their way to it, with Punch running in front as if he knew why they were going there. They climbed up to the little cave, and Nick flashed his torch above his head.

They saw the jewellery case almost at once, tucked away on a high rocky shelf. It would have been quite invisible without a torch, even in daytime, because it was such a dark corner.

Nick climbed up and got it down. It was fairly big, a nice case of brown leather. He opened it and gasped. It was full of all kinds of jewellery, including the brooches, necklaces and watch that Lydia had stolen from Holiday House. And there were the most magnificent diamonds, which the children gazed at in wonder.

"Katie, listen. I want you to go back to Holiday House and take this jewellery case to Gareth," said Nick. "Tell him that Sam has gone to frighten poor Peter, and that

I've gone after him to see what he's going to do and say."

"Oh no! Don't do that," said Katie, scared.

"Yes, I must," said Nick. "I'll take Punch with me. He might be useful. Go on, Katie, do as I tell you. I'll come and report as soon as I'm back!"

CHAPTER 15

Some Exciting Things Happen!

Nick went after Sam, leaving Katie to take the jewellery case to Gareth. How delighted he would be to see it and hear the news! Nick guessed how Sam meant to get into the old house – smash a window and climb in carefully, without cutting himself.

Nick heard the sound of breaking glass as he went up the cliff path, feeling for the sandy steps with his feet. He felt in his pocket. He didn't need to get in through the window as he had the .key of the garden door which he had taken with him after he had been to the house by way of the underground tunnel.

He opened the garden door and went in quietly, Punch at his heels. He stood and listened. He could hear footsteps going up the stairs – then loud voices!

He tiptoed up as far as the main landing and then listened to what was going on up on the top landing. Sam had evidently knocked on the locked door there and woken Peter. He was shouting at him.

"So you escaped, did you? But I've found you, and I'm telling the police where you are tomorrow, Peter, and back you'll go to the nick. That brother of yours thought he was very smart to hide you away, when you came to him, didn't he? But I'm going to look pretty smart myself, when I give the police the news of where you are. I'll probably get a reward, a big reward! And it'll pay you back for making me lose my job."

Someone answered from behind the door. "Go away, Sam. You've done enough harm to me already, I've had to take all the blame for what you did. Leave me alone and don't set the police on me again!"

Sam laughed. It was a horrible laugh that made Punch growl and Nick shiver. It must have angered Peter, for suddenly there was the sound of a door being unlocked and thrown open with a crash.

"Uh-oh!" said Sam's voice sneeringly. "So we've come out for a breath of fresh air, have we?" Then his voice changed. "Stand back, Peter. If you try fighting me you'll be very sorry!" Then Nick heard the sound of a blow, and a shout from Sam: "Don't you dare hit me or I'll show you something!"

Then there came the sound of hurrying footsteps down the stairs. It was Peter. He had dodged the blow that Sam had tried to give him in return for the one he had landed on Sam's nose, and was now running for safety. Nick was immensely surprised to see him, and so was Punch. Nick was also very scared! He turned and ran to the next flight of stairs with Punch behind him, and a most astonished Peter a few steps further back still.

Peter had no idea who Nick was. He half thought he must be a friend of Sam's, and when they came to the top of the stairs he pushed Nick roughly aside and went on down in front of him, three steps at a time.

Sam came pounding down behind him, shouting in rage. He, too, was amazed to see Nick and Punch in front of him, fleeing for their lives! Down and down they all went!

Peter ran into the kitchen, searching blindly for some way of escape. By the light of Nick's torch he suddenly saw an open

door and ran through it, not knowing that
it led down to a cellar. He lost his footing
and fell from top to bottom, where he lay
groaning.

Nick ran down the steps too, with Punch, anxious about Peter. But Sam did not follow. He slammed the cellar door shut and turned the key in the lock!

"That's you locked up!" he yelled. "It's not so comfortable as your little top room, but a night in the cellar won't hurt you! I'll bring the police along tomorrow. As for that kid and his dog, they deserve a night's imprisonment for snooping around here at this time of night."

Then there was silence. Sam had apparently gone. Nick spoke to Peter. "Look – are you badly hurt?"

"No," said Peter, who was still lying there. "No bones broken, anyway, but plenty of bruises. I'd no idea that was a cellar door I hurtled through. But who on earth are you? Not a friend of Sam's, I hope?"

"No I'm not! I'm a friend of your brother Gareth," said Nick. "I know all about you. He told me. And listen, I've got some good news for you. I know where that jewellery case is! My sister and I listened in on the beach tonight when Sam gave his sister Lydia the case, which she hid in a cave. We took it, and my sister's gone to give it to Gareth!"

"Am I out of my mind?" asked Peter, amazed, still rubbing his shins. "Will you say that all over again very slowly? I can hardly take it in, it's such wonderful news."

Nick repeated it all, adding other bits of news too. Peter gave a funny choking laugh. "I'd like to hug somebody!" he said. "I can't believe it! I suppose I'm not dreaming, am I?"

Nick gave him a polite pinch. "You're not dreaming," he said "It's all true, isn't it, Punch?"

"Woof," said Punch, and licked Nick on the cheek.

Nick shone his torch on to Peter's legs. They were certainly bruised and bleeding.

"You ought to have those seen to," said Nick, worried. "Can you walk?"

"Sure, but where to?" said Peter. "That snake Sam has locked the cellar door. It looks as if we'll be here all night!"

"I know a way out," said Nick. "Through the cellars and down an underground tunnel and out through a hole in a cave."

"You really are brilliant!" said Peter,

astonished. "I'd love to be there when your sister hands Gareth the jewellery. She must be a great girl as well."

"She is," said Nick. "Anyway, Gareth doesn't know about this tunnel. I don't think I've told him about it."

"Oh, he does know it," said Peter, surprisingly. "He must have used it when he came to the old house to hide me."

"Really?" said Nick, equally surprised. "He didn't tell me about it either! Now, can you stand? Try."

Peter tried and found that he could stand with a struggle, though it was very painful to walk. He limped through the cellars after Nick. Nick couldn't help liking him. He was older and taller than Peter but very similar to look at.

They went to the end of the cellars and came to the old doorway, the broken door beside it. Nick helped Peter down the eleven steps and into the underground tunnel.

"We go some way along and then we have to crawl up through a hole into a cave, get down on to the beach, and walk up to Holiday House," said Nick. "I do hope you'll be able to manage it."

And then a dreadful thing happened. Nick's torch flickered and went out! The battery had run down!

"Oh! My torch has gone out!" said Nick in dismay. "We'll just have to feel our way through now. I hope we don't miss the hole that takes us up to the cave!"

They did miss it and were soon completely lost in a maze of cliff tunnels. They groped along in the dark and suddenly came to a full-stop against a rocky wall.

"We've come into a blind alley," groaned Nick. "Turn back, Peter."

They turned back, and stumbled along again, both feeling scared. Peter's legs were very swollen now and he had to struggle to keep going. Punch gave a little whine.

"Go on then, you show us the way, Punch!" said Nick. "Take us back to the cellars! If you can do that we'll be safe because we'll wait there till the police come tomorrow."

And good little Punch, whose eyes could see no better in the dark than theirs, but whose nose told him the right way to go, led them safely back to the cellars, where they sat down thankfully on a big crate.

Nick wondered what Katie was doing. Was she fast asleep in bed, after having seen Gareth and given him the jewellery case – or was she sitting and worrying about him? She would have to worry all night long, then!

Katie wasn't in bed! She had gone safely back to Holiday House and had climbed up the spiral stairs to Gareth's room. There was a light under his door, so she knocked.

"Come in," said Gareth's voice wearily. Katie opened the door and went in, carrying the jewellery case.

"What's that you've got?" asked Gareth, surprised. "And why have you come to see me so late?"

"To bring you this, Gareth," said Katie, and put the brown jewellery case down on the table in front of him. "Open it!"

He opened it – and the diamonds blazed up at him.

"Katie! Where – where on earth did you get these?" he said, his voice trembling a little. "Are they – are they really the—?"

"Yes, they're the jewels that Sam took from the safe while your brother was stuffing in the vegetables," said Katie, smiling at him. "Sam was afraid for their safety in Tiddington, so he met Lydia tonight and gave the case to her for safe keeping. The other things in it are what she's been stealing, nasty little thief."

Gareth sat and stared at the diamonds, and suddenly tears blurred his eyes. This box would prove that his beloved brother Peter was not a thief! He could go free, he could return to ordinary life, and he, Gareth, could go back to school again with his head held high! He felt for his handkerchief, ashamed of his sudden tears.

"Here you are, have mine," said Katie. "I feel a bit watery-eyed too. It's all too fantastic for words, isn't it?"

"You don't know how fantastic! It's out of this world!" said Gareth, accepting Katie's hanky. "Where's Nick?" he went on. "Didn't he come back with you?"

"No, he followed Sam to the old house. I haven't come to that bit yet," said Katie. "Sam had guessed your brother was hiding in the top room there – he saw the light

161

tonight – and he's gone to frighten him. He's going to tell him he's getting the police there tomorrow to take him back where he came from!"

"That horrible man!" said Gareth, starting up from his chair. "How dare he do that to Peter! I must go and see what's happening."

"Can I come too?" asked Katie.

"No," said Gareth. "You'd better not."

"How are you going to get into the old house?" asked Katie. "And, oh, Gareth, please tell me something. How did you get back to your room the other night without our seeing you? You didn't pass the junk-room or we'd have seen you, and that's the only way into your room, past the junk-room and up the spiral stairway."

"No, it isn't," said Gareth. "There's another way. I'll show you! It takes you down underground, joins up with the tunnel that's been dug through the cliff, and leads to the cellars of the old house!"

"Oh! Then it must join the tunnel we found!" said Katie in surprise. "How did you know all this, Gareth?"

"I stayed here with a friend of mine years

ago," said Gareth, "before it became Holiday House. His mother owned the place and he showed me the old books with maps of the caves inside. Smugglers used to sail into Tolly Bay and use the caves. Goods were taken up to the ruined house and this house through secret passages. We had great fun exploring, and we found this passage – the way I'm going to use now – quite by accident! Watch!"

He went to the old fireplace and stood upright in the great hearth. He stepped sideways – and disappeared! Katie ran to the hearth. Yes, he had vanished!

It was a secret exit! So that was how Gareth had got into his room the other night without their seeing him! He had visited the old house, taking a mattress and blanket for Peter, in case he came to him for help, and had used the secret passages and tunnel to go both there and back.

Katie sat down on a chair, trembling with excitement. She couldn't go to bed. She must wait and see what was going to happen next!

CHAPTER 16

STRANGE JOURNEY – AND A HAPPY ENDING

Peter and Nick sat with Punch at their feet in the darkness of the old cellars. Peter's legs were very painful now and there was no way he could rest comfortably. He couldn't help groaning a little.

Punch went to lick him. The little dog couldn't understand this strange adventure, but he was quite happy provided that he was with Nick. He was very glad he had led them to safety.

They sat there for what seemed hours and then Punch sat up and growled. Both boys sat up too and listened.

"What is it, Punch?" asked Nick, in a low voice. Punch growled again.

And then the boys heard a noise from the far end of the cellars, where the old doorway was, leading down to the tunnel. They heard someone coming up the steps, someone walking into the cellars, someone who was carrying a brightly-shining torch.

The two boys sat absolutely still, not knowing who this unexpected visitor was. It might be that horrible Sam. Punch didn't growl any more. Instead he gave a joyful little bark and bounded off to greet the visitor.

"Punch!" said a familiar voice. "Where are Peter and Nick?"

"GARETH!" shouted the two waiting boys, and Nick leaped to his feet. Peter got up more slowly on his bruised legs.

Gareth went straight over to him and flung his arms round his brother, holding him tightly for a moment. Then he stepped back and grasped his hands. "Everything's fine now, just fine!" he said. "I've got the jewellery safely for you. Everything will be all right now, Pete. You're innocent – you'll be set free! I just can't believe it!"

Then he flashed his torch down on to his brother's legs and saw how bruised and bleeding they were.

"What a mess you're in, Pete!" he said. "Come on, follow me. Can you walk all right? I'll take you back to my room."

"Yes. I can just about walk, but that's

all," said Peter. "My legs have got so stiff with sitting. But I'm all right, Gareth, I'm fine."

Gareth led the way down the steps and into the tunnel. When they came to where the hole was that led up to the cave above, Nick stopped, and Punch bumped his nose into his leg.

"Here we are," he said. "We go up here and into that cave. I hope old Peter will be able to manage the struggle up the hole!"

"We're not going that way," said Gareth, to Nick's surprise. "I know another way which I always use when I want to return to my room!"

They went right past the hole and along the tunnel again. It twisted and turned and suddenly came to a blank wall.

"Now where do we go?" said Nick in surprise, and then, looking up, he suddenly saw a strong rope-ladder hanging down against the wall from above. He was gazing up a very narrow shaft!

"We've come to the foot of the tower," said Gareth. "We're down in the foundations. The tower has double walls just here, and this narrow shaft goes to the very top. Each of the three rooms in the tower has an entry to this shaft by way of its fireplace! It must have been seriously useful in the old days!"

Nick was astonished. He gazed up the shaft in awe as Gareth held up his torch. "Now I begin to see the answer to things that puzzled Katie and me!" he said. "That time you got into your room without our seeing you, though we waited by the junk-room door to watch for you climbing up the stairway. I suppose you entered your room by means of this shaft! No wonder we didn't see you!"

Gareth laughed. "Yes, I did. And do you remember another night, when you were outside the top tower-room – when you'd come back to get the key you'd left in the door?"

"Yes! We heard someone behind it, in the top room!" said Nick, seeing light at last. "It was you! You'd come up the shaft into that room, I suppose?"

"That's right! I heard you outside the door and grinned to myself," said Gareth. "All the same, there was no way I wanted you snooping about up there, discovering my little secrets! Now, are you ready to climb up? Pete's had a bit of rest."

"I'm ready," said Peter.

"Let's get moving then," said Gareth. "I'll go first with the torch. You next, Pete, and you last, Nick. Then we can push or pull Pete if he needs it."

"What about Punch?" said Nick.

"Can't you carry him under one arm?" said Gareth. "He's small and light, and he doesn't seem a bit frightened."

Nick picked up the little dog, who immediately wagged his tail hard and tried to lick the boy wherever he could. Gareth began to climb the swinging rope-ladder. Peter came next, finding it difficult because of his bruised legs. Then came Nick with Punch under one arm.

Up they all climbed. They passed one opening in the wall of the shaft, which Nick imagined must lead into the fireplace of the junk-room. Then they came to a second opening, and Gareth climbed through this, pulling Peter in afterwards. Nick climbed in too, and found himself on a broad ledge.

"Step down to the left, Nick," said Gareth, and Nick obeyed. Immediately he found himself standing in the big fire-place of Gareth's room! He gasped in astonishment.

A squeal of joy greeted them. It was Katie, delighted to see them. Nick introduced her to Peter. "This is my sister. She took the jewellery case to Gareth. Katie, do you know where the bandages and things are kept? We really must do something about poor Peter's legs!"

Katie stared at them in horror. "Oh! We must wake Mrs Holly. Yes, we must. He can't go about with legs as bruised and hurt as that!"

And off she flew down the spiral stairway to wake Mrs Holly.

Mrs Holly, amazed and disbelieving, took her first-aid kit and followed Katie to the tower. Peter? Who was Peter? And whatever were these children doing up in the middle of the night?

She heard the whole story as she bathed and bandaged Peter's legs. She could hardly believe it, as first one child and then another, poured it all out.

"And, Mrs Holly," said Gareth, at last, "I've got a dreadful confession to make.

Peter's not a thief, but I am! I took those things out of the fridge for Peter, because he was hungry."

"Did you?" said Mrs Holly, smiling at him. "And I suppose it was you, then, who put that money on the top shelf every now and again?"

"Yes, it was. I didn't know what else to do," said Gareth. "I felt dreadful stealing your food."

"Buying it, Gareth, with your pocket money, not stealing it!" said Mrs Holly. "There now, your legs will soon feel better, Peter. You can share Gareth's room tonight and tomorrow we will have an interesting time with the police! Goodnight, everybody! I'll see you to your rooms, Nick and Katie!"

In Katie's room, Nick began to talk about all the happenings of the evening, but poor tired Katie was fast asleep before he had finished the first sentence! Nick was tired, too, and soon Holiday House was its own peaceful self again!

In the morning, what a surprise for everyone when Gareth proudly brought

Peter down to breakfast and introduced him as his brother! Lydia, who was serving breakfast, almost dropped the teapot she was carrying. She looked scared to death. What had happened after she had left Sam the night before, and gone back to Holiday House? She couldn't imagine!

She soon knew, though, when two big policemen arrived, bringing an angry and surprised Sam with them. Mrs Holly had telephoned them and told them most of the story.

Sam was taken to Mrs Holly's room and Lydia was sent for. Peter and Gareth came in too, and last of all came Mrs Holly with Nick and Katie.

Clare longed to know what was happening. "Nobody will tell me anything," she complained to Mrs Potts. "What's going on? Who was that boy called Peter who came to breakfast? He couldn't have been Gareth's brother. Gareth hasn't got a brother. He told me so."

"Yet you said that Lydia told you his brother was a bad lot!" said Mrs Potts. "You wait and see who he really is, if you can't make up your mind, Miss Inquisitive!"

A very serious meeting was going on in Mrs Holly's room. Sam began to look extremely scared, and so did Lydia.

"We want to know what you did with that jewellery case, Sam," said the first policeman. "We know now that it was you who took it from the safe, and not Peter. What did you do with it?"

"I never took it," said Sam sulkily.

"Then how is it you gave it to Lydia for safe-keeping last night?" asked the policeman. "Nick, Katie – I believe you overheard this?"

They nodded.

"Well?" said the policeman, turning to Sam again. "Do you still say you didn't give that case to your sister Lydia?"

"I never gave it to her and she never took it," said Sam sullenly, giving Lydia a warning look. He wasn't going to admit anything.

"You hid it on a ledge in a cave, didn't you?" said the policeman to Lydia.

"I never!" she said – and then, to her horror, the second policeman silently put the jewellery case on the table. She gave a little scream, and Sam turned pale.

"I think you've seen this case before, both of you," said the policeman.

"Never! Never!" said Sam and Lydia together. The policeman opened the box. He took out the diamonds and he also took out the other things that Lydia herself had stolen. "You put these in here, didn't you Lydia?" he said. "They are the things you stole here in Holiday House."

Lydia began to sob. She broke down

completely and confessed to everything, while Sam sat and glared at her.

"Yes, oh yes! I did take those things! I did put them there. But Sam stole the diamonds in the jewellery case. He did, he did! He took the case while Peter was playing that silly trick, stuffing the headmaster's safe with the vegetables. Sam made me say I was with him at the time of the robbery, he made me!"

"I see," said the policeman. "So Peter here is completely innocent, it seems. Sam tricked him into playing a stupid joke, and stole the case himself. Is that it, Sam?"

Sam made no answer. He sat and glared first at the sobbing Lydia and then at the table.

"Take them away," said the first policeman to the other one. And Sam and Lydia were duly removed to a police car outside in the drive.

"You can go, children – and you too, Peter and Gareth," said Mrs Holly.

They all went out, looking rather sober and serious. It was very satisfactory, but not very pleasant, to get hold of wrongdoers.

Clare came up. "What's it all about?" she

demanded. "Is he really your brother, Gareth? You told me you hadn't got one!"

"I made a mistake," said Gareth gravely. "I find I have one after all. A very special one indeed!"

"Oh, I'm glad," said Clare. "And you do look different, Gareth, sort of relieved and happy."

"Do you know," interrupted Peter, smiling round suddenly, "it's my birthday today! I'd forgotten it till now! Well, I certainly feel like having a birthday, I must say."

Mrs Holly came up, smiling. "Your birthday!" she said. "Oh, good, Peter! First we'll go and buy you some birthday presents, beginning with some new clothes, and then we'll all have a wonderful lunch somewhere. Then we'll come back here and swim, and we'll end up with a picnic down on the sands, with everybody invited, even Vicki's baby brother."

"I'll ask Mrs Potts to ice the big new cake she made yesterday!" said Clare. "And I'll help you to make all the sandwiches, Mum!" She raced off happily, longing to tell the great and most surprising news.

"You are kind," said Peter to Mrs Holly. "I'd like a good birthday, I really would, after all those miserable months when everyone thought I was no good, just a mean, despicable thief!"

"Forget it," said Gareth. "Many happy returns of the day, Pete – sorry I forgot!"

"Mum!" shouted Clare from the bottom of the hall. "How many candles, Mrs Potts says – for the birthday cake, I mean!"

"Seventeen!" shouted back Peter. "I'm getting very old indeed. I hope Mrs Potts has enough candles for me!"

After a wonderful day, everyone from Holiday House joined in Peter's birthday picnic by the sea. He blew out the seventeen candles on his magnificent cake and grinned broadly at Gareth, Nick and Katie, as the sound of "Happy birthday to you!" rang out over Tolly Sands.